I0672138

THE WARRIOR

BARRETT BOYS #5

JORDAN FORD

FLP

© Copyright 2021 Jordan Ford
www.jordanfordbooks.com

———

All rights reserved. This book or any portion thereof may not be
reproduced or used in any manner whatsoever without the express
written permission of the author.

———

This is a work of fiction. Names, places, businesses, characters and
incidents are either the product of the author's imagination or are used
in a fictitious manner. Any resemblance to actual persons, living or dead,
actual events or locales is purely coincidental.

———

Cover Design © Niki Ellis Design

———

ISBN: 978-1-99-115134-6 (Paperback)
ISBN: 978-1-99-115135-3 (Kindle)

Forever Love Publishing Ltd
www.foreverlovepublishing.com

I dedicate this book to anyone who lives with deep regret.

"Forgive yourself. The supreme act of forgiveness is when you can forgive yourself for all the wounds you've created in your own life. Forgiveness is an act of self-love. When you forgive yourself, self-acceptance begins and self-love grows."
~ Miguel Ángel Ruiz Macías

1

AN ISLAND HIDEAWAY

Cooper

THE SUN IS A BLAZING orb in the sky, drenching the island with afternoon light and warmth. The palm trees, rustled by the soothing breeze, and water so clear you can see your toes on the ocean floor, make *Paradis Idyllique* the picture-perfect getaway.

Which is why things are crazy busy all year round, particularly from November through to the end of January. As one group leaves, another arrives. It makes those transition days freaking hectic as we all bustle around cleaning rooms and making sure our "first impression" is one to remember.

I don't mind it so much. I love the energetic, frantic

buzz. It keeps me busy, and that's way better than lying around with nothing to do.

I squint up at the clear blue sky, stretching for mile upon endless mile, and figure that the resort manager, Maurice, will be internally happy-dancing over the weather. I'm sure he prays to the weather gods every time we get a new group in, but some groups are more important than others, and a boat full of wealth is heading to the island right now.

We waved off a group of retirees this morning. I was a little sad to see them go. Twelve couples, all suffering from empty-nest syndrome, had decided to use some of their hard-earned savings for a week of luxury. They had a blast on the island—snorkeling, sunbathing, reading in the cabanas, and drinking cocktails at sunset. They were a fun group, good for a laugh and not too wild.

I highly doubt the luxury yacht arriving this afternoon will be carrying the same type of people. From what I've heard, it's a bunch of rich college kids probably avoiding snowy Christmases with their families.

An image of snow-covered mountains and fields pierces me, my chest shuddering as I see myself next to the cozy fireplace and feel the warmth of unwrapping Christmas presents like I was a normal kid with a normal life.

But it was all just a dream—a time in my life that I somehow knew would come to an end before I was ready for it.

Gritting my teeth, I push the thought out of my head and focus back on work. I've cleaned the pool, straightened out the deck chairs, swept all the staircases leading down to the beach. The loose board on the pier has been secured, and the faulty chain above the swing chair has been replaced. I've rechecked every hammock to make sure there are no tears or weaknesses, especially the two that stretch right off the deck and over the water. The last thing on my list for now is to check the contents of the activities shed to make sure all the snorkeling gear and paddle boards are in good shape. That'll take some time, but I've got about an hour before the boat is due.

Because the resort is guest-free right now, I take a shortcut between the bungalows and round the corner to find Bembe and Jazz taking a "kissing" break. Her cleaning cart is forgotten, her smooth brown legs on full display as her uniform is hitched way too high, so Bembe can explore the hills and valleys of her rounded body.

"Shouldn't you be doing that in the room, where you can't get caught?" I cross my arms, resting my hip against the cart.

Bembe laughs into his girlfriend's mouth. "If we go into the room, man, there'll be nothing stopping me from taking all of her clothes off." His Caribbean accent is thick, giving the words a joyful flair.

I can't help laughing while Jasmine lightly slaps his arm. "Put me down, you fool."

She unhooks her ankles, and he lowers her to the ground, planting one more kiss on her mouth before she's free to turn back to her job. A red hue darkens her skin as she avoids looking at me.

I snicker and she glances my way, her sharp look shutting me up.

These two are always getting busted making out. They're like horny high schoolers, but I guess they're still in that loved-up, obsessive phase of their relationship. They got together over the summer, which is a blessing all of its own. I was getting so sick of Bembe whining in my ear about how much he liked Jazz but didn't want to ruin their friendship.

In the end, she finally made a move, and the biggest battle now is trying to keep their hands off each other.

"If I walk away right now, will you guys be able to get the rooms cleaned by the time our guests arrive?"

Jazz flushes again, and Bembe curls his arm around her shoulders, kissing her neck lightly and whispering something I try not to hear.

She turns to him with a smile that says it all, kissing him full on the mouth before slapping his butt. "Be gone. Stop distracting me."

With a little flick of her hand, we're sent on our way and only moments later are bumping into Kingston, who is carrying a stack of boxes to the kitchen.

"Need a hand?" I grab the top one and divert course, figuring it'll only slow me down by a few minutes.

"Thanks, bro." Kingston gives Bembe an expectant look, and the tall guy next to me sighs before grabbing the other box so we've all got one.

With a cheerful grin, Kingston leads the way through the meandering paths and around to the back of the kitchen. It's the noise that hits me first, followed by a smell that makes my stomach yearn.

Juan, our head chef, will be pulling out all the stops, and I can already tell that tonight's meal is going to be a good one. We're not allowed to eat it, but sometimes if we're lucky, we'll get leftovers the next day.

I wait for my turn to set the box down, then rub my hands on the back of my shorts and get ready to head to the activities shed.

"So, I heard this boat is a party cruise." Kingston's broad smile makes me pause. "No doubt filled with rich assholes and hotties in skimpy bikinis."

I roll my eyes and go to leave again, but Kingston grabs my arm before I can. The guy's always been chatty. It's mostly about himself, so it doesn't bother me too much.

"We might finally get you laid, brother."

"Stop it." I scowl, while Bembe cracks up laughing, clapping his hands and dancing around with glee.

"Never gonna happen." He shakes his head. "You know we can't get busy with the guests."

"Doesn't stop me." Kingston's arrogant smirk is almost punchable, but he's... well, he's Kingston. The guy is all cocky show and bravado, but beneath all that BS is a happy, lovable guy who I can never stay mad at for long. "There are plenty of places to hide on this island, little pockets of privacy where anything can happen... if you know what I mean."

Great. Now he's wiggling his eyebrows at me.

"I'm not into girls like that," I mutter.

"What, hot females with fine bodies?"

"No, girls dripping in wealth and privilege. They swan up to the bar, flirting their asses off and expecting you to drop to your knees and drool at their feet."

"Everyone who comes to this island is like that."

"Not the last group we just had."

"They were like our grandparents." Kingston pulls a disgusted face.

"And not families."

Bembe starts laughing. "Don't you be telling us those rich mamas aren't flirts. They're the worst."

"Yeah, maybe, but I still think a boatload of families is better than college party animals," I admit.

"No way." Bembe shakes his head. "Crazy-ass kids running around? No thank you! At least this way, we get delicious eye candy."

I jerk to face him with a deep frown. "You've got a girlfriend. And she is gorgeous."

"I know. I know. She's my one and only, man."

Kingston laughs. "But it's hard not to admire the beauty of God's creation, right, brother?"

He slaps Bembe's hand, and they both start grinning like idiots while Bembe admits, "That's all I'll be doing."

I roll my eyes again and walk off before they can pull me into any more conversations about rich hotties and skimpy bikinis.

We have plenty of them come through here, and the odd woman's caught my eye, but none have turned my head.

Bembe obviously doesn't realize how lucky he is. Jazz is great. She's funny, full of energy and life. She kind of sparkles no matter what she's doing, and he can't tell me beauty is worth more than that. I'd rather be with a girl who can make me laugh than one who just looks good all the time. I don't give a shit about any of that shallow appearance stuff. Give me depth. Substance.

Give me…

I shake my head, reminding myself that I'm not really interested in that either. Women complicate everything. I just want to stay focused on my simple island life. I don't need much—give me work, sun, and plenty of the outdoors. That's all I want.

My feet slow as I approach the boat shed and am pierced by yet another image from my past. Wavy blonde hair, gentle green eyes, and a laugh that was pure music.

It floats through my head—loud and wonderful—until reality snatches it away from me. That girl is gone. Like everything else in my past, I'm never going to see her again. And that's probably the way it should be.

2

PARADISE FOR CHRISTMAS

Ashlyn

I REST my forearms against the railing of the yacht and gaze out at the water. Seabirds float and glide above the surface, a light breeze playing beneath their wings. Sun heats my skin, and I close my eyes, lifting my chin so it can soak me.

Yes. This is perfect.

Christmas on an exotic island. My parents didn't even mind me going. They were heading to Vale for a ski-cation anyway and simply shrugged when I told them I'd rather hang out in the sunshine with my friends.

"Whatever you want, sweets."

They've been saying that to me most of my life, and I

guess that's the easier way to live. Mom and Dad have always been travelers, flitting off whenever work would allow them to. As Dad's business grew and he was able to step back a little more, they started leaving for longer periods of time. Sometimes they'd take me with them… or they'd send me to stay with relatives. It was hard not to resent it, although I won't complain about Montana.

Never Montana.

That place was…

"Hey, party girl." Leo and Shira swan up to me, tipsy smiles on their faces.

I blink, my thoughts disintegrating as. life on this luxury yacht suddenly comes back into focus. The thumping music upstairs that seems out of place in this setting makes me blink, and I have to force a smile as my two best friends approach me.

We've been rooming together since sophomore year, and I love them both so much.

"What are you doing hiding around here? There's more food to be eaten, and Chanel's trying to start a little dance party on the upper deck."

I snicker, picturing the brunette with her tightly covered curves breaking out the moves to impress Paul or Hugh… or maybe both.

"Selfie!" Shira holds out her phone, and we gather close to snap one of her daily million.

That's what Leo and I call them. I swear, it feels like she's always snapping photos. Her Insta account has a massive following, and although I love her content, I don't understand why so many others do. It's just us. Her friends. She's pulled the window to her life wide open, and the public seems to love it.

"This is so cute! Mind if I post?"

I nod like I always do. At least she asks our permission. Although, I wonder if she'll even be able to post. We've been warned that there's no cell service on the island.

"Do I look good?" Leo moves behind me so he can look over her shoulder. "Oh yeah, I do. Post away, baby."

"Island getaway, here we come." Shira talks while she types. "Christmas in the sun, bitches! See you on the other side."

Leo whoops and wiggles his hips, bumping into mine and trying to get a smile out of me.

"Did it post?" I ask Shira.

"Yeah, the boat has reception, but once we get dropped off on the island, we're going dark." She winces, biting her lip like this is actually a crisis.

I can't wait. Switching offline for a while? Yes, please. I'm not even sure why it appeals to me so much. I guess I just need a break from… everything.

"Seriously, girl, why are you hiding back here?" Leo runs his hand down the back of my hair.

"Just…" I shrug, then give in because the look on his face always makes me fold. "Hiding from Varam." I cringe and await their reactions.

Shira snorts and starts laughing while Leo wraps his arm around my shoulders.

"You know he basically planned this trip just to get you to a private island, right?" Shira shakes her head.

"That boy wants to see you in a bikini. He wants to show you how freaking rich he is."

"His daddy is the rich one," Leo adds with an eye roll. "And Varam wants to woo your ass. You know that. If you don't want him to, then why did you agree to come?"

"Because it's a freaking private island in the Caribbean." I give him an exasperated look. "Sun, heat, warmth, luxury. How could I say no to that?"

"You managed to say no to Florida for Thanksgiving." Shira's pointed look makes me dip my chin.

"That was different," I murmur, not wanting to go in to it. I've hardly divulged anything about my trip, which is so unlike me. The three of us usually tell each other everything, but the harsh disappointment of Cooper not being in Montana was too much. I just couldn't tell them.

The stupid thing is, I *knew* he wasn't going to be there, but when Aunt Nell said Barrett Boys, my heart started singing and it wouldn't freaking stop. I had to visit. To see for myself.

It was so surreal seeing Cooper's brothers all grown up. We sat for hours that night, talking about all they'd been through. They're men now, which means Cooper's a full-blown man too. The oldest of them all, he'll be twenty-three by now. It's been over five years. I should be totally over him.

Why does he linger?

Because you never got closure.

Damn him for leaving the way he did.

"I still don't get it." Shira nudges my elbow. "We had a

blast in Miami while you froze your ass off in cowboy land."

"It was nice to see Aunt Nell again." I shrug, wondering if I'll have to repeat my carefully manufactured explanation of why I bailed on my buddies.

"Plus you didn't have to spend the holiday fobbing off Varam." Shira giggles, but her laughter quickly cuts off.

"Incoming," Leo quietly sings in my ear.

I stiffen, gripping the railing and pasting on a polite smile as Varam and Lance wander over to us. They're both holding beer bottles and looking relaxed. Open shirts display lean bodies that have been carefully built at the gym. Appearance is everything to guys like this. I'm pretty sure Shira told me Lance actually gets his chest waxed because he likes that smooth, movie-star look.

I glance at Varam's smooth, brown skin, guessing he probably does the same.

"Here you guys are." His smile is broad and cheesy.

I don't know why, but I've always found it a bit too wide, too big, too… plastic.

Is that mean?

His teeth are so straight and have been whitened so they look like veneers. Everything about him is just too perfect. He's like an Indian Ken doll, and it bugs me.

"So, what are the three amigos discussing?" Lance drops a kiss on Shira's lips. He's so much taller than her, she actually has to go on her tiptoes whenever she wants to kiss him.

It's kinda cute.

I love these two together.

I just wish Varam wasn't going to be Lance's best man at the wedding… whenever that ends up being. I'm pretty sure Shira wants to graduate before they set a date.

Varam smoothly eases his way between Leo and me so our arms are pressed tightly together. I shift to my left, but I can't go too far without muscling into Lance and Shira's kiss, so I'm kind of trapped. Desperation sears me, and I berate myself for saying yes to this trip. Are sun, heat, warmth, and luxury really going to be worth this?

"You know what? I feel like we need cocktails." Shira glances at me, her eyes twinkling before she turns to Lance. "Baby, will you come help me?"

"Sure." He grins, running his hand down her back.

"And, Varam, what's that recipe you gave me last time? It was so delicious. I think Ashlyn loved it too. Right, Ash?"

I pick up what she's doing and quickly nod. "Oh yeah. It was refreshing and kind of tangy."

Varam's chest puffs with pride as he stands tall and snaps his fingers. "The Varam Vodka special. VV for short." He laughs.

"Could you make us some of those?" Shira's voice has that fake, sticky edge to it. I never like it when she does that, but it's amazing how often it works.

"Of course I can." He grins, shooting off to the bar area with Lance and Shira in his wake.

"I'll try to stretch it out for you," she whispers as she passes me.

"You're an angel."

She winks and wraps her arm around Lance's waist.

My shoulders slump with relief, and I hang my head. This is going to be a long ten days. Varam convinced everyone to extend it so we could see the new year in.

"Once we get to the island, we'll spread out and try to block for you," Leo promises.

"Thank God for you two."

"I still don't know what your problem is. Varam's a hottie."

"Just because someone's hot doesn't make them the right person for you. He's just… not my type."

"Gorgeous, rich, intelligent. Ew, who'd want to get with that? I see why you don't like him."

I snort and nudge Leo's elbow. "If you think he's so hot, why don't you go for him?"

"He doesn't swing my way, sweetness." Leo pouts for a second.

I wrap my arm around his shoulders, kissing his cheek. "We'll find a man who is perfect for you."

"Scott was," he whispers, his pout turning into a deep frown.

Scott and Leo dated for about a year, but then Scott broke it off when things started to get too serious. Leo was dropping the L-word and hinting at moving in together. It freaked Scott out.

None of us expected him to be a commitment-phobe, and Leo was devastated. We've been trying to cheer him up for about six weeks, and he's doing much better, although he still drops into moments of uncharacteristic silence.

"Are you sure you shouldn't just call him?" It's the

same question I ask every time he gets this look on his face.

Leo shakes his head. "He wanted space, so that's what I'm giving him."

"But you still miss him so much."

I know that feeling, not that I've ever admitted it to Leo. But I do know the pure torture of pining for someone you can't have.

"It's all right." He shakes his head, his voice breaking as he tries to put on a brave smile. "The island doesn't have reception anyway."

"How will Shira cope?" I raise my eyebrows and make a funny face.

Leo gives me a half-hearted laugh.

With a glum smile, I admit, "Heartache sucks."

He rests his head against mine, and we wallow for a few minutes before he pulls in a breath and stands straight. "I won't let it taint this trip. We're in paradise! For Christmas! My broken heart is not going to ruin anything. We need to party hard, dance late into the night, and wake up hung over. It's the only solution."

I giggle.

"And if I just happen to wake up next to a gorgeous, naked man, then so be it."

My laughter grows. "You're going to know everyone on the island. Do you seriously want to get with one of these guys?" I tip my chin up to the noisy chatter and thumping music above us.

"Island resorts have staff, Ashlyn. There's bound to be some smoking hot cabana boy that will make my wildest fantasies come true. Don't kill my dreams, babe."

My heart goes all mushy as I stare at my friend. I love the way he talks, moves, sings. He's a ball of energetic fun, and I couldn't ask for a better bestie. "I adore you, Leo."

"I adore you more. Now look at that sparkling water and marvel. We're in paradise, girl. We must marvel."

"Okay." I stare at the rippling water below us, the salty air filling my nostrils as I breathe it in. I force myself to soak in its beauty, noticing the diamonds of sunlight on the water and the rush of the ocean as the boat cuts through it.

It will be easy to marvel here. This place is stunning, and the pictures on the *Paradis Idyllique* website were amazing too. We're in for a vacation of pampering, partying, and getting a wicked tan. I should be the happiest girl on the planet right now.

"Where are those cocktails?" Leo mutters. "We need sustenance."

He wanders off, and I should follow him, but instead I stay put for just a few more blessed minutes. I don't know why I'm feeling so restless. It's been hard to shake for a while now, and maybe that's why I went to Montana instead of Florida this Thanksgiving.

What is wrong with me?

I should be stoked that I'm here, experiencing this. All these people... these *friends*... who I've spent the last four years partying with. I'll know everyone on the island. It's going to be freaking awesome.

But is it?

Is Varam the only thing getting me down?

I close my eyes, rubbing my forehead and knowing that's not true.

It's not just Varam. Although the guy is clueless and refuses to believe I'm not into him, I can handle it.

It's just…

"Montana." I breathe the word like it's a special brand of oxygen.

It was always my happy place.

Those summers were magical. I lived for them. Aunt Nell always made me feel so special. I loved the mountain views, exploring the forests on horseback, sneaking away to make out with Cooper.

A smile curls my lips, an electric buzz firing through my body.

I loved him.

Yeah, I was only a teenager, and some might call it simple infatuation, puppy love, an immature crush.

But my heart knows different.

Cooper Barrett wrapped his beautiful soul around mine, and I'm not sure I'll ever fully get over him.

Maybe going to Montana for Thanksgiving was my biggest mistake. Being back there stirred it all up again. I'd managed to shut my pain away in college, distract myself from the loss, but then I stupidly returned and it's like I have to start all over again.

So start! Do what you did last time.

I'm not going to ruin this trip. I'll be staying in

paradise, surrounded by luxury and my friends. I can't let this chance pass me by.

The sad truth is... I'm never going to see Cooper again.

I just have to get over it.

Standing tall, I slap the rail and take in a deep breath.

Time to put my party-girl pants on and make the most of this trip.

"You can do this, Ash. Just smile like you always do."

Pasting on a wide grin, I let the thumping beat from upstairs run through me and start swaying my hips, heading for cocktails and a dance with my friends.

3

MAURICE'S GOLDEN BOY

Cooper

WITH THE ACTIVITIES shed looking neat and organized, I head back to the main entrance. Maurice just radioed everyone to let us know the boat is pulling up to the pier now. Bembe and I are on luggage detail, as per usual. The group is about twenty strong, so it shouldn't be too bad, although with the amount of luggage these people sometimes bring, we could be in for a workout.

I shake my head with a grin, thinking about my one backpack that has taken me through multiple states in the USA, down through Mexico, and finally landed me here. It's been over five years, and I've never needed more.

Picking up my pace, I duck around the back of

Bungalow Two and come face-to-face with my boss, who is walking to the pier at a fast clip.

"Oh good, I was just about to radio you." He points the walkie-talkie at my chest while smoothing down his salmon-colored tie. In spite of this being an island, he always wears a suit and tie. The guy's a classy Frenchman, and first impressions mean a lot to him. "The hand basin is acting up in the women's bathroom."

"Which one?"

"The restaurant. It's about to be filled with guests, and I don't want them needing the washroom and finding a leaking tap. Can you quickly see to it? I'll help with the luggage today."

"Sure thing." I hurry off to grab a tool kit.

I'm no plumber, but thanks to Maurice always coming to me first, I've become the resort's go-to handyman. The staff sometimes hassle me about being Maurice's golden boy, but I'm pretty sure the reason he always starts with me is because he knows I'll say yes without hesitating.

I like to keep busy, and missing my scheduled time off doesn't usually bother me very much. It means when I'm really desperate for a run or a hike to get away from everyone, Maurice will always make it happen for me.

Yeah, maybe I am his favorite.

I grin, grabbing the tool kit and heading for the ladies' rest room, which is situated in the back corner of the restaurant. I take the back route, around the admin block and past the kitchen. I'll walk down the pathway where only staff go so the new guests don't see me.

"Hey, Cooper." Gisele skips up to my side, her long

pigtails bouncing. She's one of the resident children on the island. Living here with her parents and two brothers, she certainly brings a playful edge to the happenings around here. Considering there are only three kids living at the resort, I think she does pretty well. It must kind of suck being the only girl around. That's why it's so cool when we get a group of families through. Gisele and her brothers have a blast.

"Hey." I grin.

"Can I help?"

"Aren't you supposed to be at school?"

"Home school finishes at one o'clock, dummy. It's nearly four."

Wow. This day has flown. I glance at my watch, wondering why I even bother wearing it. I hardly ever check the time. My day is divided into tasks, and I keep track of the hours by my jobs, knowing how long each thing will take and what I can fit in between meals.

"How was school today?"

"Wonderful!" She stretches her arms wide.

I chuckle. "You never say that."

"It was wonderful because tomorrow is Christmas Eve and I don't have to do any schoolwork for fourteen whole days!"

"Me either! Me either!" Tajo comes running up, taking a nosy look at my tool kit and pulling out a hammer before I can stop him.

I quickly snatch it back and tuck it safely away. That boy cannot be trusted. His imagination turns twigs into machetes, nails into darts, and last time he had a hammer, he thought he was Thor. It didn't end well, and his poor parents had to shell out to replace the sliding glass door in Bungalow Eight.

"Children!" Amani pops out of the kitchen, sweat beading her brow as she dries her hands on her apron. "Leave poor Cooper alone. He has work to do."

"We're helping!" Gisele protests.

"No! Get in here. *I* need your help."

"Aw, Mama."

"Don't you whine to me. Get your butts in here. You can wash some dishes."

Gisele's lower lip sticks out, and I lightly rub her back. "You can help me next time." I wink at her, and she flashes me an adoring grin before chasing after her brother.

I snicker and shake my head. Ever since I met Gisele, she's been trailing me around, trying to help me with jobs in order to get out of school or chores. Her mother won't let her get away with it, and I'm quietly grateful. If Gisele had her way, she'd be attached to my hip. I'm pretty sure she's got a ten-year-old crush that only seems to be growing. I try to be nice to her without being overly friendly. It's a weird balance.

It helps that her brothers are never too far behind her, so I'm able to interact with all three. They're great kids, always up for a laugh and some fun. The boys love to tussle with Bembe and me. When the beach is free, we'll play soccer with them and try to keep them entertained to give their hard-working parents a breather.

The kids have relatively free rein on the island, which

drives Maurice crazy, but Amani and Juan are good parents, and the kids are often found working in the kitchen with their mom and dad.

Juan's one of the best chefs in the Caribbean, but he's got one condition—he comes with a family. The owner of the island, Monsieur Beauchamp, told Maurice to make an exception. He wants *Paradis Idyllique* to be known as one of the top resorts in the world. As long as the children are out of sight when guests are around, then they're able to stay. We quietly make an exception when it's a family group, but when it's a bunch of grown-ups looking for an adult-only experience, then those kids become invisible.

We call it Ninja Time, and it helps the kids keep a positive attitude about it.

The three of them are pretty good at sticking to the rules and staying in the staff-only areas most of the time. It's when the island is in between guests that they run wild, setting all their pent-up mania free.

I snicker again, trying to imagine what it must be like to raise three kids in this environment. Some days it must be like trying to contain wild monkeys.

Turning the corner, I walk the back pathway and slip into the bathrooms from the service entrance side. I smile briefly at Kingston and Tash, who walk past the bathroom alcove carrying trays of pretty drinks with little umbrellas to welcome the guests.

The steel-drum band has already started playing calypso music, and I shut the door on the sound, rushing to fix the leak before any guests walk in.

4

A WHITE SUMMER DRESS SPELLS IMMINENT DISASTER

Ashlyn

BY THE TIME we reach the island, I'm feeling more relaxed. One VV special and a watermelon martini have probably helped, so when I step off the boat, I'm feeling a light, happy buzz.

"This place is amazing." I gaze ahead at the cute bungalows scattered amongst palm trees on a land of lush greenery that slopes down to a sandy white beach.

The jetty we're walking down leads to a wide staircase and up to a vast deck littered with places to soak in the sun—swinging chairs, hammocks, wooden loungers. If I'm remembering correctly, the pool starts on the left and goes around the corner to a manmade waterfall and a drinks bar so you can sip your cocktails from the water.

"Eeeeee!" Leo squeezes my arm and starts happy dancing.

"Bonjour! Welcome to *Paradis Idyllique*." A woman with a bright smile and rose-red lipstick greets us at the bottom of the stairs. Her hair is pulled back into an elegant bun, and she's holding a clipboard. "My name is Rowena, and I will be your hostess and activities director while you're on the island. Any problems, I'm here to help." She has a slight French accent, but it's mingled with an American twang on some of the words. "Please, follow me to the restaurant for a complimentary cocktail and further details of how we will make your stay as luxurious and memorable as possible."

She leads us up the stairs and past a band who are welcoming us with groovy island sounds that make my hips sway. I smile at the members, my eyes skirting over the steel drums, bongo, shakers, bass guitar, and trumpet. They grin and boogie to the music, obviously loving this as much as I am.

Shira lifts her arms and starts shaking her hips, dancing her way into the open-style restaurant. The walls are thick plastic that have been rolled up to allow the ocean breeze to waft through. The ceiling above us is decorated with tropical-style artificial flowers, a fresh pop of rainbow colors to contrast with the dark wooden floors and thick beams that border the restaurant. Waitstaff circulate the room with friendly smiles as we find seats at the shiny wooden tables. They deliver cocktails with umbrellas, along with cubes of fresh pineapple and mango on toothpicks.

"Oooo." Leo takes two pieces of pineapple and runs out of hands to take a drink. The waiter smiles at him and places the fancy-looking beverage on the table. "Thank you." Leo giggles and does his flirty eyes.

The waiter gives him a polite smile, then turns to me.

"Piña colada, miss?"

"Yes please." I take the drink and bypass the fruit, internally groaning when Varam pulls out the last seat at our table and winks at me. He has his phone out, filming this all with running commentary.

"And here is the restaurant, filled with luscious ladies." He wiggles his eyebrows at me, and I turn away so he can only film the back of my head. He says something else I'm too annoyed to soak in and then laughs.

"You know there's no Wi-Fi on the island, right? When are you planning on posting all this footage?" Leo asks him.

"When the boat comes back to pick us up in ten days. I'll just have a bunch of TikToks in draft and post away."

"Nice." Shira giggles. "I'm totally going to do that too."

"I managed to post my last video just as we pulled in, showed off the luscious island, and then told my followers I'd be offline. They'll be hanging out for content by the time I return."

I roll my eyes and share a subtle look with Leo. My tipsy friend gives me a sloppy grin before popping a piece of pineapple in his mouth and looking like the giddiest guy in the room. Yeah, he really needs to ease up on the drinks.

The calypso music finishes with a flourish and we all cheer the band, whooping and hollering in our excitement. The buzz in the room is pretty freaking high and electric, and it takes Rowena lots of throat clearing into the microphone to get our attention.

"I'd like to introduce you to the resort manager, Maurice."

A dapper-looking man in an elegant pinstripe suit steps forward with a polite wave.

Rowena glances at her clipboard and continues, "We are here to make your stay as perfect as it can be. Tonight we welcome you with a first-class island meal, prepared by one of the best seafood chefs in the world. This luxury buffet will be served from seven o'clock in this area. After that, you can make your way to the bar." She points to her left and I sit up, peering out of the restaurant and across to a large wooden decking area, plush outdoor furniture creating corners in the space. I can't see the bar from here, but the string of lights wrapping up the palm trees and bordering the square tell me it's going to look freaking magical at nighttime. The ocean breeze will be hitting our skin, and I bet the inky vastness of the view will be amazing. The moon will sparkle over the water, stars twinkling in the distance.

This place is freaking Utopia!

"Drinks will be served until midnight, and you can dance the night away to live music from our calypso band, Sunshine and the Dragonflies."

Another cheer goes up. The band waves and grins, the guy on the steel drums doing a little roll.

"And just as a reminder, everything on the island is included in your luxury vacation package except for the alcohol. You can open a tab at the bar and pay this at the end of your stay. Are there any questions?" A beat of silence and no raised hands leads her to a quick finish. "Fantastic! For now, we will get you organized into your rooms. The staff are delivering your luggage as we speak and will return to guide you to your allocated bungalow. If you have any problems or concerns, please ask any of the staff you see wandering around the island. We are here to make your stay as perfect as it can be." Her smile is bright, and you can tell she's said this speech a hundred times before. "Now, before you leave this area, for your own safety, I must go over a few rules and regulations we have on the island."

I grab my drink, watching the lady talk and not noticing how full my glass is.

"Oh shoot." I lurch forward as the bright liquid splashes onto my white summer dress.

"Always." Leo gives me a pitiful frown. "Girl, I can't take you anywhere."

"Shut up." I laugh, lightly slapping his shoulder and knowing he's right.

I seriously have an inability to keep my clothes clean.

Why I chose to wear a white dress is beyond me, but it was perfect for an island getaway, and I put it on as soon as we landed in Saint Martin this morning. I look pretty hot in it. Shira said so, and I didn't even think about spillages until I started eating lunch. I was extra careful and didn't spill a drop.

Until now.

Looking over my shoulder, I spot a sign for the restrooms and slip out of my chair, heading for the back corner of the restaurant. Rowena's voice carries across the space, and I listen with half an ear about the areas where guests are not permitted before ducking into the alcove and walking toward the wooden female sign on the bathroom door.

When I push it open, the first thing I notice is a pair of legs—muscular calves with a fine coating of blond hair and manly feet shoved into a pair of well-loved flip-flops. Worn khaki shorts sit perfectly on his hips, and I can't help admiring the curve of his firm behind before the humiliating realization hits me.

Oh crap! I've walked into the men's room!

But then I spot the tool kit, and the maintenance man spins around to face me...

And my world goes still.

What?

I'm frozen.

"Sorry, ma'am, I won't be—"

His voice cuts off, much like the air in my lungs. He gapes at me like he's seeing a ghost. All I can do is stare at him, my lips slightly parted, my heart thrumming out of control.

Cooper?

I take in his tanned skin and his wild crop of sun-kissed hair. He looks like an island man, his dark beard and shoulder-length waves nothing but… gorgeous. Sexy. He's grown so much, his rugged beauty only enhanced with age.

And his face…

I used to run my fingers all over that face, exploring every curve and crevice, running the tip of my thumb down his straight nose and over those perfect lips. It'd always make him smile, and then he'd kiss me.

He clears his throat, his Adam's apple bobbing as he swallows and turns to wipe out the porcelain basin.

"I won't be a minute. I'm sorry to have startled you. I should have put a maintenance sign up."

His voice is clipped and efficient.

My forehead wrinkles.

Why isn't he saying my name or hello even?

Does he not recognize me?

I try to catch his eye in the mirror, but he keeps his chin tucked down and won't look at me.

I keep staring at him, wondering what to say.

"Hello" might be a good start.

But I can't even form that simple word.

It's Cooper!

My Cooper.

The man I never thought I'd see again. He's standing three feet away from me, and my racing heart is telling me it has to be him.

I lick my lips, my tongue like sandpaper all of a sudden.

"There you go," he murmurs, grabbing his toolbox and angling his body so he can pass me without us touching.

I step aside. It's an automatic response I have no control over.

It's not until the door swings shut behind him that I'm able to blink and take my first real breath.

Leaning against the basin, I stare into the mirror, taking in my bulging green eyes and pale complexion. Lightly touching my windblown hair, I finger the ends and try to make sense of this.

Maybe it was just some kind of weird mirage.

Have I drunken too much?

I did have a few cocktails on the boat. That piña colada from the restaurant must have gone to my head, right?

No! You were too busy spilling it on yourself to taste any of it.

I glance at the stain on my white dress but can't move to wash it.

My hands are shaking. I'm not even sure how I'm going to turn the faucet on. The one Cooper was just touching. I reach out and run my fingers over the shiny brass.

"Cooper." I whisper his name like I have a million times before.

He's the wish I make before I blow out my birthday candles. The dream that only comes to life when I'm sleeping.

Snatching my hand back, I rub my forehead and try to pull myself together.

This can't be real.

"Just an illusion. It must have been the watermelon martini that tipped you over the edge," I tell my reflection.

"You're drunk." My laughter is short and punchy, cut off by a blatant thought I can't ignore.

You're not drunk! You just saw Cooper and he didn't even know who you were.

My expression crumples.

My Cooper would. He'd know me.

So maybe it wasn't him.

Surely that has to be the best explanation. Because if he did know me and just acted that way, then that's just brutal.

Closing my eyes, I dip my head and let my long hair fall over my shoulders.

What am I going to do?

How do I manage this?

If that man is Cooper and he knows me but is choosing to ignore me... that *hurts*.

But if it's not Cooper and just some guy who looks exactly like him, then that's a whole new torment of its own.

I think my perfect week in paradise has just been totally trashed.

5

OFF-LIMITS

Cooper

I WALK OUT of that bathroom as calmly as I can until my body can't take it anymore. As soon as I hit the staff area, I break into a sprint, the toolkit slapping against my leg. The second I reach the maintenance shed, I slam the door shut behind me, letting the cool darkness shroud me as I rest against the workbench and suck air into my lungs.

Why isn't it working?

Why can't I breathe?

You just saw Ashlyn. It was Ashlyn!

My Ashlyn.

Damn, she looked amazing.

She's a woman now.

The last time I saw her, she was about to turn seventeen… and now she's… Shit, she'll be twenty-two now. Her birthday is just before Thanksgiving. I remember, because I used to send her a card every year with a letter that was probably way too long for a guy to write. But I couldn't help it. I'd pour my heart and soul onto those pages, and she'd lap it up. I knew those words would be safe with her, because she understood me like no one else ever had.

"Ashlyn." I whisper her name, pain searing me as I grab my mouth and fight this unexpected urge to cry.

Blinking, I stand up straight and suck in a few more mouthfuls of air, my mind wandering back a decade, to the first time I ever laid eyes on her.

The sun was a fireball, and I wiped sweat off my brow like I was a man and not a fourteen-year-old kid trying to wield an axe.

Not trying. I was, dammit.

I was using this axe and feeling like a freaking king. It was the first time Grandpa had let me, and I was taking honor in this job.

A tree had fallen on the west edge of the property, right near the fence line. Grandpa wanted to use it for firewood over the winter, and we were chopping it up into manageable, transportable pieces. He'd taken Brody and Deeks back with the recent load, and I was staying behind to keep hacking at the tree. Michael and Jake were on housework and kitchen duty that afternoon. At least dinner was going to be delicious. Michael cooked the most out of everyone, because he loved it so much and it kept everyone else happy. The nights we were rostered on, to give him a cooking break, were never as nice.

My stomach growled just thinking about what awaited me after this hard labor.

I raised the axe and brought it down with a loud *thwack*. The branch started to crack beneath the force, and I hit it one more time before using my boot to kick it free of the trunk.

Man, it was hot.

Summer was definitely here, and as much as I loved the warmth and blue skies, it got near boiling during tasks like this one.

I wiped my forearm across my forehead again. Drops of sweat trailed down my skin, racing for first place to my chin and neck. With a sniff, I lifted the axe once more but stopped when I heard the sound of galloping hoofs.

My heart stuttered, my body tensing as the sound came closer.

Shit.

Nell never rode this far from her house. It must be a stranger. Strangers asked questions; they might talk, spread gossip. They could tell someone that they spotted a boy at the Barrett ranch. Questions could be asked, news might spread to Florida, and then Dad would find us.

No! That couldn't happen!

I was two seconds away from jumping down and

hiding behind the tree when I caught a glimpse of the rider.

I couldn't hide fast enough, but then... I kind of didn't want to.

She was young—well, maybe my age—her light, reckless hair jumping around her shoulders as she bounced in the saddle. Wow. She was pretty. That smile could reach me a mile away. She was the definition of happy... and I was spellbound.

She spotted me and blinked with surprise before pulling the horse to a stop. It whinnied and shook its head but was obedient to her touch. This obviously wasn't her first rodeo. She seemed calm and in control of the large animal. I glanced at its shiny brown coat, but my eyes were drawn back to her face only moments later. I was a moth, and she was the flame. It made me helpless.

I had to gaze at her, study her pretty features. Her long, oval face with the pointy chin, her cute nose, those sparkling green eyes that held me captive.

What the hell was wrong with me?

I'd seen girls before!

But not her. You've never seen her.

"Hi." Her smile grew even wider. I didn't know it was possible, but it made her even prettier.

I swallowed, wiping my brow yet again. I didn't know what else to do.

I hope it looked cool.

It probably didn't.

You're dripping with sweat. You look like you've been freaking crying or something.

Adjusting my backward cap, I managed to nod at her and maybe smile? I couldn't tell what my lips were doing. They felt kind of useless and frozen.

"I'm Ashlyn." She leaned forward in the saddle, like she wanted to get a better look at me. "What's your name?"

"Coop… Cooper."

She nodded, her cute expression filled with fun and curiosity as she lightly held the reins and redirected the horse when it started eating grass through the fence line. She turned him sideways so he could munch on the grass without fence wire in the way.

"I've never seen you around here before."

"I haven't seen you either." I shrug, nerves scattering through me. Not many people saw us here, because we couldn't allow that. My grandfather kidnapped us to keep us safe, but the law probably wouldn't see it that way. But if he hadn't taken us, Dad never would have let us leave. And without Mom there to try and protect us, who knows what he would have done. He'd given me enough bruises and even a couple scars that would last me a lifetime. I couldn't stay with that evil man. None of us could. So we let Grandpa take us, because it was the only way.

"I'm staying with my great-aunt Nell." Her nose wrinkled and she looked around, squinting against the bright light. "Guess I don't usually ride this far away from the house, but she said I could take a couple hours to explore as long as I didn't cross onto anyone else's property."

My insides settled and I nodded.

Aunt Nell was safe.

She knew her next-door neighbor, Ray, was looking after his five grandsons since his daughter had passed away, and she didn't seem to need more information than that.

"Is this the Barrett ranch?" the girl asked.

I looked down at the axe, not sure what to say. Grandpa had warned us not to be too open with strangers. It was for our own safety, and all of us had happily agreed. We hardly ever saw anyone anyway.

Looking back up at the pretty girl, I shaded my eyes against the sun and asked, "Where are you from?"

"New York." She shifted in the saddle, her smile sweet and open. "Manhattan, actually. That's why my parents like to send me out here every summer, so I can get a real taste of nature."

I liked the sound of her voice. It was bright and friendly, like listening to joy, and it reminded me of Mom in those rare happy patches when Dad wasn't being an asshole and she was just enjoying the peace for a while. "Do you like it here?"

She tipped her head to the side. "It's pretty good. I like the forest… and the mountains are beautiful… and it's fun riding and exploring." A giggle broke up her words. "Yeah, I love it."

Again, her smile grew, and it was soon competing with the sun or maybe butterflies or wildflowers or any of the most beautiful things I could think of.

She tipped her head the other way, her gaze studying me. My chest started to feel weird. This warm, tingly sensation was traveling through me. I kinda liked it.

"It does get lonely sometimes. Summer can be long when you're the only kid in the house. All of my friends are in New York, and…" She brushed a lock of hair off her face. "I mean, Aunt Nell's great. Uncle Thomas can be a little scary, though."

I couldn't help a soft laugh. "Yeah, he's a grumpy bastard when he wants to be." I cringed, suddenly realizing I shouldn't have said that, but Ashlyn cracked up laughing like it was the funniest thing. Jumping down from her horse, she ran her hand over his sleek neck and approached the fence.

"I like you." She nodded, and for some reason, the action drew me to her. I stepped my sweaty ass off that tree trunk, laid the axe down, and approached the fence as well.

I didn't even think about how bad I might smell. All I could see was her and the mesmerizing way her nose wrinkled as she asked me her next question.

"Think we could be friends? Maybe we could hang out some time."

Yes! All the time! I would hang out with you anywhere, any day, anyhow!

I managed to contain my excitement into one simple word. "Sure."

She grinned again, and that tingling sensation turned into an electric buzz.

She captured me that day and hasn't let go since.

I've always thought about her, dreamed about her. Shit, it's probably the reason I've never been that interested in dating. Girls have come on to me over the years, but none of them have been Ashlyn, and it's pretty hard to fall for anyone else.

She's like the Oscar of females, the Pulitzer Prize, the gold medal. How can anyone else compete with that?

"And she's here. On the island." My whispered words sound more like a croak.

The weight of that reality is concrete in my stomach.

What am I going to do?

I thought I was as far from my past as I possibly could be, and now it's just waltzed right back into my life, slapping me in the face while simultaneously igniting all those little love bugs again, the ones that kept me company throughout my teenage years.

"Ashlyn." Her name is the sweetest-sounding, sweetest-tasting treat, but…

It's also forbidden fruit.

I can't.

I can't go there again.

It wouldn't be right. Not after what happened… what I did.

I don't have the luxury of reminiscing, flirting, any of that stuff. She is off-limits.

Scrubbing a hand down my face, I squeeze the back of my neck and wonder if it's plausible to spend the next ten days hiding in the maintenance shed.

6

UNREQUITED LOVE

Ashlyn

THE BATHROOM MIRROR starts to blur. I have no idea how long I've been staring at it, but my heart is still thundering to the point of feeling nauseous.

I can't hide in here forever, though.

With trembling fingers, I manage to wash my hands, forgetting why I was even in the bathroom to begin with.

When I step out of the room and find Leo and Shira waiting for me, I actually yelp.

"Are you okay?" Shira giggles.

Leo's face pinches with concern as he grabs my hand and gives it a little squeeze. "You look like you just saw a ghost."

"I did," I rasp, blinking and trying to figure out if I want to cry or scream or... I don't know what I'm feeling!

"Oooo." Leo peeks around me, eyeing the bathroom door like an apparition is about to float through it. "Tell me everything."

His wiggling eyebrows and fun smile fade quickly when he looks at my face again. Touching my cheek, he's back to concern.

"Come on, girl. Let's get you to our bungalow."

"I'm coming too." Shira's voice is unusually quiet, her face a mask of worry. "Let me tell Lance and I'll meet you there. What's your number again?"

"We're in four."

Shira rushes off to find her fiancé while Leo leads me to the bungalow we'll be sharing. We don't say anything as we walk the meandering paths. I should be marveling at the beauty around me, but all I can see is Cooper. He flashes from the young teenage boy I fell in love with to the man who just ignored me in the bathroom.

It can't be him.

But it is!

"Here we go." Leo walks us into a divine bungalow that's been purposely designed to look natural and authentic yet carries all the mod-cons of a luxury getaway.

For a moment, I'm taken by the stunning view.

We walk through a short corridor, the door to the bathroom on our left, and then pop out into an open, airy bedroom with two luscious double beds and a comfy sofa that faces out to the ocean. One entire wall is sliding glass doors, giving me the sensation of standing on the edge of the beach and looking out to the vast ocean beyond. It stretches for miles, eventually blending into the sky.

"This *is* paradise," Leo softly sings as he spins around, running his fingers over the bright orange and yellow cushions adorning the couch. The beds are white linen, crisp and made perfectly, with towels in the shape of swans and bright flowers covering the end.

"Okay, I'm here!" Shira rushes in, checking my face before yanking me onto the couch.

We sit in a huddle, Leo perched on the wooden coffee table so he can face us.

"You're still pale. Start talking." Shira pats my hand.

I blink and glance between them.

I've never told them this stuff before. I've never told anyone... except Aunt Nell. She held me when I cried over Cooper's mysterious departure.

For some reason, from the first day I met Cooper, I knew I had to keep him a secret. I didn't figure out why until our third summer together and he admitted the truth about his dad and how they ended up on the ranch. I swore I'd never say a word. It made us closer somehow, and from that point on, our friendship became something more intimate. I was fourteen the first time he kissed me.

A thrill races through my body. I can still remember his touch so clearly. Even after all this time, he's never let go of my heart.

And now he's here!

I sniff, tears scorching my eyes.

"Ash, sweetie. What's happened?" Shira runs her hand down my back.

"He's here," I whisper.

"Who's here?"

"This guy who…" I suck in a breath.

My friends both wait with bated breath, leaning in close like I'm about to tell them a national secret.

"His name was Cooper—*is* Cooper." I'm flustered and have to flap my hand through the air. "I met him in Montana. I used to spend my summers there when I was a kid."

"With your aunt Nell."

I nod at Leo and keep going. "I was twelve when I met him, and we hit it off really quickly. I used to *live* for my summers. He'd write me on my birthday every year and I'd write back, and we just… we fell in love."

Shira sighs with a dreamy smile. "Teenage love."

I want to correct her and say "*forever* love," but I can't quite do it.

I lost Cooper… at least I thought I did.

"So, what happened?" Leo rubs my knee.

"Well, he…" I blink. "About five-ish years ago, his grandpa died, and I don't know all the details, but he just took off. Left Montana… and didn't even say goodbye. He was gone, and he so obviously didn't want to be found."

"Sweetie." Shira tucks a lock of hair behind my ear. "That's awful."

"I never thought I'd see him again." I sniff, the tears getting that much harder to fight.

Threading my trembling fingers together, I rest them on my lap, but it's too hard to sit still, so I start messing with the fabric of my dress.

Leo runs his hand down my arm. "I can't believe you haven't told us this before. The look on your face right now. Your voice. Is he like the love of your life or something?" His romantic heart must be going crazy right now.

I give him a weak smile. "I don't know if I've ever really gotten over him. It broke my heart to lose him, and I had no idea what he was doing with his life. I mean, he could have been dead, but… somehow I knew he wasn't," I whisper, staring at my fidgeting fingers and feeling my heart flutter. "I just… I couldn't bring him up, you know? It was too painful."

Leo forgives me with a kiss to the cheek. "But he's here now."

"Yeah." I shrug and my eyes start to water again. "I saw him in the bathroom. He was fixing the sink."

"And…" Shira's brown eyes are so expectant. So hopeful.

I slump with a sigh. "He acted like he didn't know me."

She pings straight, an angry scowl morphing her features. "What!"

"Yeah, he just stared at me for a minute, and I thought he recognized me, but then he looked away and politely apologized, working fast to finish up. He left without even looking at me again."

"Unbelievable!" Shira's hoop earrings swing as she shakes her head.

"Maybe he doesn't realize it's Ashlyn." Leo runs a calming hand over Shira's knee, then looks at me. "You said it's been like five… six years, right?"

"Yeah, true." Shira's still frowning. "I mean, I guess. But it's still kind of rude. How can you forget the love of your life?"

"Maybe I wasn't his love." My spine curls, my entire body sinking as that awful thought hits me.

"No. Stop that." Leo points his finger at me. "Maybe he's just in shock like you are. He thought he'd never see you again and bam! There you are. You have to talk to him."

I give him a dubious frown.

"At least find out if it really is him." Leo flicks his hand in the air. "Once we know that, we can work from there."

I bite my lip, unsure if I really want to venture down this path.

Revisiting those blissful summers might only cause me pain.

He left!

He didn't even care enough to write me a letter or say goodbye. He just took off.

What if I really did mean nothing to him?

But you did! Those birthday cards, those letters. He loved you, Ashlyn.

"Not enough to find me," I whisper.

"What was that?" Leo leans his ear toward my mouth.

I shake my head. "Nothing."

With a thick swallow, I force my gaze to the stunning view. I don't want this week to be ruined by unrequited love. I'm here to have fun with my friends.

Dammit, Cooper! Why'd you have to be here?

I knew a small part of him would always stay with me,

but I had hopes of moving on. Now after just one awkward interaction, I'm back to that agony of knowing how much I still care.

Holding my head in my hands, I let my hair fall on either side of my face and hide within its shelter.

Leo and Shira are kind enough not to say anything.

Instead I get wrapped in a group hug, which I'll quite happily stay in until I can figure out what the hell I'm supposed to do.

7

SERIOUS TROUBLE

Cooper

THE LIGHT through the window of my studio apartment is pale, casting a soft glow over my unmade bed and revealing dancing dust particles that look way too happy and relaxed to be here.

I sit at the table, nursing a bottle of cheap beer and staring into my gloomy room. I hardly ever hang out in here. This place is for sleeping, reading, showering... and that's about it.

When I do get time off, I always leave the resort to explore the island, find secret water holes to jump in or small beach coves to hang out in for the day. I'll take an old boat out fishing or just find a perch on the highest point to stare at the view.

But I don't really have time off today.

I'm supposed to be helping out around the island, but instead I'm taking five… ten… forty minutes to hide away and figure out what the hell I'm supposed to do.

I've just come face-to-face with my past. Images of Ashlyn swarm me, from the twelve-year-old girl I first met to the luscious woman she was becoming before I split. Her beautiful face is interrupted by thoughts of my brothers, everything from the sound of their unchecked laughter to their terrified pain.

My father was an asshole.

He took everything from us.

And I hated him for it.

My chest constricts and I lean forward in my chair, resting my elbows on the table and holding my head. My brain wants to explode.

A gunshot rings out. So final.

The looks on my brothers' faces. Pure shock. Disbelief.

Our old man was dead.

And our beloved grandfather was dying in Jake's arms.

I couldn't fix it.

Tears needle my eyes. It hurts as I fight them back, blinking and sniffing.

Taking a long pull of beer, I drain the bottle and slump back in my seat, picking at the label with my thumbnail.

I need to cut these thoughts off. I can't relive the past again.

Shit, what if Ashlyn finds out what I did?

She used to adore me. I could tell every time we were together. It was mutual, but I never had the courage to tell her. And then I became… well… I killed a man.

She deserves better than that. Everybody I love does.

Closing my eyes, I ward off the memories of running away. It was ten past three in the morning as I snuck out Aunt Nell's window and made my escape.

It was the right thing to do, but guilt clung to me—a suffocating, heavy cloak that I've never been able to shake.

"I have to get off this island." I bolt out of my chair.

I can't face Ashlyn and what I did to her or my brothers.

It was the right thing to do, but it still caused pain, and I've moved on with my life now.

I can't go back.

Throwing the empty glass bottle into my recycling box, I fling the door open and leave the staff housing quarters in search of Maurice. I'll tell him I'm sick.

That won't work. You're never sick.

I'll tell him I have a family emergency.

You don't have a family, dumbass!

The thought is a blade through the gullet. I keep walking, my brain swimming with plausible excuses, but none of them are good enough.

"Hey, Coop."

Someone calls my name, and I lift my hand in greeting but don't soak in who it is.

I have to find Maurice, and I have to find him now.

I head straight for the reception area, which is the only place on the island housing telephones and technology.

Cell reception is basically nonexistent, but the office has ways of reaching the outside world. I kind of love that. This place has been perfect for hiding away and forgetting about life on the outside.

But now life has shown right up on my doorstep, and if I have any chance of surviving, I have to escape her.

"Maurice around?" I ask Rowena.

She's sifting through paperwork and glances up from the desk. "Actually, I think he's looking for you. He tried radioing before, but you didn't answer."

"Crap," I mutter, remembering how I'd turned my radio off and thrown it onto my bed.

"Try the restaurant. I think he's overseeing setup for dinner."

I tense. "Are any of the guests in there?"

"I don't think so." She looks confused by my question. "I'm pretty sure they're down on the beach, which is where you should be, right? Or is Bembe on duty this afternoon?"

She goes to check her roster, and I quickly skip out before she can tell me off for shirking my responsibilities.

Running for the restaurant, I nearly crash right into Maurice as he walks around the corner.

"Cooper." He grins. "I've been looking for you."

"Yeah, I wanted to speak with you too. Any chance—"

"I need you to cover for Rocco tonight. He's come down with something and needs a replacement pronto."

I clench my jaw, swallowing down my now futile request. Like he's going to let me get off the island before this group leaves.

"He's tending bar now but looking pretty green." Maurice winces. "I know you're not scheduled to work tonight, but if you could pick up this extra shift, I'd be really grateful."

I never refuse this man—that's why he always comes to me first—but I still give it a try. "Can't Kingston or Tash? They've both got skills behind the bar."

Maurice's eyebrows flicker with a frown. I never try to get out of things. "They're already covering food and tables. I need you, man. I know it's an extra shift, but please. Help me out."

"Yeah, sure." The reply slips out of me, an automatic response that I can't control.

"I knew I could count on you." He slaps my shoulder and leaves, his steps fast and purposeful as usual.

With a resigned sigh, I run a hand through my hair and make my way to the bar.

It's happy hour before dinner and will no doubt be swarming with guests who are hyped up to party hard on their first night at *Paradis Idyllique.*

I scan the crowd as I walk along the edge of the dance floor and around behind the bar. I don't see Ashlyn, which is a huge relief. It helps me breathe easier, and I actually smile when Rocco spins to see me.

"Oh, thank God," he murmurs, wiping his sweaty brow.

Whoa, the guy does look very pasty.

"Take off, man."

"You're a life saver." He slaps my shoulder.

"Go sleep off whatever's kicking your ass. I'll see you in the morning."

He's already walking away and calls over his shoulder, "I owe you."

"No you don't." I shake my head and grin at him, then turn my attention to the two guys leaning against the counter and perusing the drinks menu.

They end up ordering two beers, and I add the expense to their bungalow tab, which Rocco already started.

The pre-dinner drinks session goes fine, and while the guests linger over an extravagant buffet meal in the dining hall, I take a few minutes to scarf down some food in the kitchen before heading back to the bar.

By the time guests start trickling back in, the bar is fully stocked and ready to go. Sunshine and the Dragon-flies have already started playing, and it draws the crowd quickly. I'm pretty sure every guest at the resort is soon packed into the area... including Ashlyn Smulders.

The second she appears, I'm hyperaware of her every move.

Right now, she's sitting on one of the low couches, surrounded by her friends and smiling at the short one with mountains of dark brown curls surrounding her face. She's expressive and talks with her hands, her large engagement ring catching the light, along with the other expensive-looking bracelets and rings adorning her skinny fingers and wrists. An Asian dude is sitting with them, wearing chic white pants and a bright pink shirt. He's all style and obviously very close to Ashlyn, the way she's sitting next to him. His arm's around her shoulders and he keeps whispering into her ear, making her grin and giggle.

A pain in my chest vacillates between an ache and a sharp jab. I try to avert my gaze and stay busy fulfilling drink orders, but my eyes keep tracking back to her.

She's so freaking gorgeous, just the way I remember her, yet not. She's older, sexier somehow. The floaty dress she's wearing hugs her body in all the right places. The plunging neckline goes all the way to her waist, where it's pulled tight by this band thingy and then floats down to her ankles, like she's wearing a shimmering sunrise rather than fabric. The bottom part has a huge split in it though, so when she crosses her long legs, the fabric drapes around her, revealing those toned, tanned calf muscles and thighs.

Stop looking or you're going to start drooling!

She always had great legs. Damn, I loved those legs.

I can feel my fingers running over them. Her smooth, silky skin. Those little summer shorts she used to wear. The frayed denim would tickle her upper thighs, and I'd be mesmerized by the way they hugged the curve of her butt. She'd jump into my arms, wrap those long legs around my waist, and I was gone. She could have asked me to do anything, and I would have.

I place a cocktail on the counter and politely smile. "There you go."

The girl takes the martini glass and gives me a flirty grin.

I'm completely unaffected by it, the way I usually am.

Girls don't tend to capture me... because there's only ever been one.

And she's sitting over there with her luscious waves of golden hair and her big hoop earrings. They lightly tap her cheeks when she shakes her head and then laughs at something Mr. Pink Shirt said.

A surprising jealousy tears through me, and I have to turn my back on Ashlyn and her boyfriend. I assume that's who he is.

Of course she has a boyfriend. She's beautiful, funny, kind, friendly—the perfect girl. She had no reason to stay single, that was just my choice... because I couldn't get over her.

Gripping the counter, I take the next order with a forced smile, willing my hammering heart back to its normal rate.

It's only the first freaking night of her stay and I'm already a hot mess.

Yeah. I'm in serious trouble.

8

RECON IN A PINK SHIRT

OH, this is bad.

I am in so much trouble.

Cooper's at the bar, looking sexy as hell, and I'm gone. All those old feelings are back with a vengeance. Not the anger and hurt over him leaving but the good stuff... like how much I used to love being with him, talking to him, kissing him. How I'd race from Aunt Nell's house to our secret spot in the woods, where we'd spend hours making out and laughing together.

I yearn. I pine!

You perish.

I snap my eyes shut and will the emotions away, trying

to focus on Leo's voice in my ear. He's being extra funny tonight, and I'm sure it's an attempt to distract me. Shira and Leo are on a mission to make sure the vacation isn't ruined by my mysterious past. That's, of course, countered by the fact that they desperately want to know everything. I know it's taking all their willpower not to hunt the island for him so they can see what he looks like. I told them I just wanted to enjoy dinner and not think about it.

Of course eating was nearly impossible, but I'm putting on a bright smile and laughing as much as I can... while trying not to check out the bar every two seconds.

My friends haven't spotted Cooper yet, but my lack of eye control has just killed my grace period.

"What do you keep staring at?" Leo finally asks, spinning around to seek out the one thing I'm trying, and failing, not to notice. "Is that him?" He gasps, turning back to me with bulging eyes. "The bar tender with the short ponytail, trimmed beard and... and body like Adonis?" His voice goes wispy and I'm sure he's imagining what Cooper looks like under that shirt right now.

"Stop it," I grumble.

Leo beams at me. "Holy hot one, girl, he is gorgeous."

A grin curls my lips before I can control it. Ducking my head, I tuck a lock of hair behind my ear. Great, are my hands shaking again?

I drop them into my lap and try not to fist the delicate fabric draping over me.

Just be cool.

Leo's openly ogling him. "You sure he's straight?"

"He was the last time I knew him." I grip his arm and force him back to face me. "Would you stop staring like that?"

Leo shrugs. Unperturbed by my reprimand, he spins around to look at the bar again. "People change."

Shira laughs. "Aw, Leo, honey. You getting yourself a little crush?"

"How can I not? He is scrum-diddly-umpscious. I've always had a thing for guys with long hair like that. You know this about me, ladies."

I can feel my cheeks blazing, because Leo's right. The way Cooper's grown his hair out… and that beard. He was always gorgeous, but now he's even more so. He *is* scrumptious. And I bet he still feels just as divine as he did back then. Memories flood me—his hands, his lips, his strong arms holding me against him. Heat flashes through my body, followed by a tug on my heart that's almost painful.

Shira wraps her arm around Leo's shoulders. "Baby, we're gonna find you the right guy, but that hotcake behind the bar belongs to Ashlyn."

"No, he…" I shake my head and sigh. "That was a long time ago."

He's probably moved on by now. Why wouldn't he?

It's been years!

He's probably got some hot girlfriend.

Who wouldn't want a guy like Cooper?

He's sweet, intelligent, thoughtful, kind… not to mention mouth-wateringly beautiful. He's probably got a long line of ladies begging to go out with him.

Maybe that's why he acted like he didn't know me. Because he's, you know, totally in love with a gorgeous Caribbean babe who is funny and smart and makes him laugh and he can tell her anything.

They probably live together. She no doubt works on this island too, and they're planning on getting married and having babies and living out all my fantasies!

I squeeze my eyes shut, my stomach surging with hot bile.

"Hey." Shira leans over Leo to squeeze my arm. "He might still be yours, and there's only one way to find out."

My eyes creep back open and I stare at my friend, her eyes sparkling with encouragement.

Leo jumps up and straightens his shirt. "I'll go do some recon."

"What? No! Leo!" I snatch for his arm, but he's moved out of range. Panic skitters through me as he flounces over to the bar, but I don't want to jump up and grab him. It'll just make a scene, and it was hard enough explaining myself to my two best friends. I can't tell everyone else! Talk about a nightmare.

"Crap," I mutter while Shira runs a soothing hand down my arm and cringes.

"Let's hope he behaves himself."

I scoff softly and clench my jaw. With my breath on hold, I await the pending exchange, taking in every little detail like a hawk. My heart is racing, my mind a whirlwind of questions and what ifs.

Dammit. I hate feeling this way.

I shouldn't!

Cooper left his family without a goodbye. He ran out on me and our summers together like they meant nothing!

I should be furious with him.

But as I gaze across the fairy-lit room to the man behind the bar, all I can see is… my first love.

The calypso music fades to white noise; the crowd, the dancing, the chatter—it's a blur. The only thing that comes into crystal-clear focus is my Cooper.

The guy who stole my heart and never gave it back.

Clutching the couch cushion beneath me, I watch with bated breath as Leo grabs his attention and does a little recon.

9

ONE GOAL. THAT'S IT.

Cooper

MR. PINK SHIRT approaches the bar with a bounce in his step and a determined look on his face.

Here we go.

The guy was sitting with Ashlyn.

She must have told him about me.

Damn, what did she say?

Was she angry? Furious? Hurt?

Let it be anger. The idea of hurting her kills me.

My throat gets thick and gummy when he rests his hand on the bar and snaps his fingers to get my attention. He already had it, but I was acting busy at the other end of the bar, kind of wishing he'd go away.

But I can't ignore him. Maurice would kill me and then want to know why I was suddenly doing a really crappy job of tending bar.

Clenching my jaw, I head over and force a smile. "What can I get you tonight?"

"Tequila shots please, good sir."

"How many?"

"Let's make it six."

He flashes his pearly whites at me, and I nod, grabbing the shot glasses and a bottle of tequila.

"So, you been working here long?" The guy leans on the bar like he's trying to flirt with me. The lusty sparkle in his eye and the way he's checking me out make my forehead wrinkle.

A microsecond of confusion skitters through me, but then I suddenly realize that I'm reading all the signs right.

This guy is gay.

Ashlyn's boyfriend is gay.

Which means they aren't together. They're just buddies.

Relief.

It floods my chest like I've opened a dam or something.

Crap. I have no right to feel that way. Ashlyn isn't mine anymore. I forfeited that right the second I walked away.

Glancing at his expectant face, I fill the shot glasses and murmur, "A while."

"I can tell." The man's eyes run up and down my body

again. "Those tanned arms. You must spend a lot of time in the sun."

"I love the outdoors." I force another smile, loading up a tray with the shots, lime wedges and a saltshaker. I slide it over to him. "Which bungalow are you in?"

I jot down the number and find his name in the computer—Leo Zhao—then start up a tab for him and the girls.

"So, Mr. Bartender, do you have a name?" His fingers curl around the edge of the tray, but he's not moving away until I give him an answer.

I know what stubborn determination looks like. I lived with Jake until he was fourteen. That kid had it down to a freaking art form.

Jake.

Damn, he'll be nineteen by now. I pray he's in college and doing well. He was always the smartest person in the room. I hope like anything that he's doing something good with his brain.

My chest tightens and starts to hurt as I wipe my hands on the back of my shorts and nod. "Coop Adams."

I pick my birth name. As much as I hate the connection with my father, it'll separate me a little more from Ashlyn. She only ever knew me as Cooper Barrett. The moment we started living on Grandpa Ray's ranch, I took his last name and claimed it as my own. The less association I had with my old man, the better.

Coop Adams might throw Ashlyn off. It might make her doubt that she knows me. Maybe she'll talk herself into thinking that I just *look* like her summer fling from years ago.

If I keep acting aloof and clueless, then she'll realize I'm not the guy she used to know.

That's what I need her to do.

Because I'm seriously not that person anymore.

The night my dad showed up uninvited to the ranch, I became someone else. And that someone doesn't deserve an Ashlyn Smulders in his life. She's way too good and pure. Way too perfect.

My old life has to remain in the past.

Scratching my chest, I ignore the searing pain and move to the other end of the bar, smiling at the gorgeous girls who have just stepped up to place an order.

Focus, Cooper. Remember who you are.

That's right.

I'm just a guy who works on an island resort. I'm here to make the guests smile and ensure they have a good, safe time on *Paradis Idyllique*.

That's my only job this week.

My only goal.

Nothing more.

10

FRESH WAVES OF PAIN AND UNCERTAINTY

Ashlyn

THE STEEL DRUMS trill as Leo hurries back with the drinks.

Handing me a shot glass, he bulges his eyes at me and then slumps with a sigh.

"Is he single?" Shira asks, licking her hand and then sprinkling a little salt over her skin.

"I didn't ask that." Leo hands me a shot. "My recon was to find out if he was in fact Mr. Summer Romance." Grabbing the shaker, he copies Shira, and they down their shots together before grabbing a lime wedge each and sucking it.

Shira winces, then laughs while Leo drops the wedge

and rubs his fingers together. Looking at me with a sad frown, he rubs my knee and pouts. "I'm not sure he's your guy. His name's Coop Adams."

"Coop is short for Cooper." Shira gives him a pointed look, then downs her second shot, wincing as the alcohol no doubt burns through her.

She giggles and sucks her lime, turning with a squeal of surprise when a sure hand slides down her bare arm.

"Hey, baby," Lance whispers, his expression drunk... but I think on love.

That guy is so gone for Shira. It's the sweetest thing ever. He's always adored her, and she eventually fell. Now she's as loved-up as he is.

"Wanna dance with your man?"

"You know it," she purrs, taking his hand and leaving me stranded on the couch as Varam quickly approaches. He looks just a touch nervous, and from the look he shares with Lance, it's obvious he's been pumped up by his best buddy to ask me to dance.

Crap!

I wish I could say no.

Let me sit on this couch and wallow over the fact that Cooper gave Leo the wrong name. He was never a stupid guy. If he'd wanted to be remembered, he would have told Leo that his name was Cooper Barrett. Although, Adams does have a familiar ring somehow. And Cooper wasn't a great liar. He had too much integrity. If he couldn't tell me the truth, he just wouldn't say anything. If I ever pushed too hard, he would get up and walk away, and then I'd have to chase after him with an apology. His eyes would lose their guarded edge, and he'd pull me against him.

"There's just things… I can't talk about."

"I understand." I'd smile and his hands would glide around my waist. "But if you ever want to tell me anything, you can. Nothing you say will ever make me change my mind about how great you are."

He'd give me a dubious smile but then kiss me, long and sweet. It was his way of saying thank you, and I didn't mind it one little bit.

I knew what Cooper wanted me to know, and that was okay because I trusted that whatever he *did* say was the truth. That was a million times better than someone who spun lies just to keep me happy.

Cooper was always authentic. It was one of the things I loved most about him.

So why the hell is he lying now?

Unless he changed his name after he ran away.

Or he's become someone you don't know anymore.

I kind of hate to concede that the boy I fell in love with might be a different person now. Something triggered him to ditch his family. Maybe he's not the guy I always loved.

Maybe I should just let this whole thing go!

But he's right there, and I'm desperate to know why he took off. He would have been grieving his grandpa, but it seemed so extreme to abandon his brothers the way he did. I'd love to know his thinking, but I doubt I'll ever find out. He obviously doesn't want to connect with me again, so maybe I should just go dance with Varam. Maybe get a little drunk and try to push Cooper freaking Barrett out of my mind.

Downing the shot, I stand up and teeter after Varam. His enthusiasm over my acceptance is kind of off-putting, and I'm second-guessing myself the minute we step onto the dance floor.

He rests his hand lightly on my waist, but I step back, lifting my arms and giving myself room to move. My hips sway to the beat, and I give Varam a tight smile as he steps back into my space and copies me.

Yeah, I think I'm gonna need more alcohol.

Glancing over my shoulder, I send a silent SOS to Leo, who immediately jumps up and lets out a whoop, dancing toward us and turning the duet into a trio.

Thank God!

I feel instantly better the second he's near, and I start to relax. Leo has been my godsend so many times. When I first started college in New York, I was still grieving the loss of Cooper. I didn't go to Montana that summer, heading to Europe with my parents instead. They quickly tired of my moping and threatened to send me home early if I didn't start enjoying the luxurious trip. I tried but quickly failed and ended up asking them to send me home.

By the time college started, I'd been packed for a couple weeks and was more than ready to go. I met Leo on the first day, and he pulled me into his circle of friends. I found a new family among them, and in spite of how restless I've been feeling lately, I will always love them. Well, especially Leo and Shira.

Ugh. I seriously need to get over myself.

I'm surrounded by fun-loving party people. I'm on an exotic island. I should be euphoric! Why can't I just accept what I have and live it up?

Glancing over my shoulder, I use the excuse of a spin to check out Cooper again. I make it a 180 turn so I can face him for a moment. He's smiling at Teagan and Mel as they order a round of cocktails.

That smile.

It's still the same, tipping a little higher on the right, his serious eyes crinkling just a little at the corners.

I can't help staring at him the way I used to. He always captured me, from that first day I saw him chopping up that tree. It's like we were meant to meet, to fall in love. I used to believe it was cosmic. We were soul mates, destined for eternity.

But I was wrong.

I mean, obviously.

He used to be able to sense my gaze. Would turn from across a field and spot me. I was his homing beacon, and he was mine. We didn't need words. Distant stares were enough. I mean, sure, we could talk the hours away, but we also had the ability to just be silent together. Hands and eyes can talk too. His eyes were always a tractor beam to my soul.

I used to think it was mutual, but he hasn't even noticed my perusal tonight.

Whatever we had has died.

And I'm grieving all over again.

11

CHOICES AND CONSEQUENCES

Cooper

IT TAKES everything in me not to stop what I'm doing and find Ashlyn on the dance floor. She's looking at me. I can feel her gaze.

It makes my stomach shake, but I'm able to hide it while making cocktails. Taking my sweet time, I stare at the wall of liquor and refuse to turn around. She'll have no idea how badly I want to connect, how every fiber of my being is telling me to turn the hell around and make eye contact. But I won't let myself do it. It's best that we don't remember those summers on the ranch.

Fighting my instincts this way is damn hard, but I can't give in.

I have to be strong for her… for me.

Tipping the liquor into a martini glass, I place the final flourishes on the drink and walk it over to the girls.

"Thanks." One of them gives me a demure smile and winks.

I pretend I don't notice the gesture and start wiping my hands on the towel hanging from my waistband.

My eyes betray me, skirting over the floor and spotting Ashlyn. She's turned and is facing the tall Indian guy. I don't like the way he looks at her. It makes my skin itch.

I thought Leo might have been a problem, but it's actually the tall guy eyeing up Ashlyn like he wants to eat her or something. His expression is the definition of lust. My muscles coil, my forearms tightening as I make a fist beneath the towel.

It should be me on that dance floor.

Well, not really. I hate dancing, but I'd like the chance to hold her again. Memories of her body pressed against mine whistle through me, and a yearning I haven't felt in years flairs to the surface.

Stop it!

"What can I get you?" I focus on the man in front of me. He orders three beers, and I grab the bottles from the fridge, uncapping them before placing them on the bar. Punching in his details, I keep his tab going and turn to the next customer, happy to be kept busy.

In spite of myself, my gaze tracks to the dance floor in regular intervals. I need to know where she is, which spots of the room I should avoid looking at, and okay, I want to know she's all right.

The second wave of relief that punched through me when her friend, Leo, joined them on the dance floor almost made me light-headed. The tall guy was a little perturbed. His expression told me so, but Leo ignored his dark look and stayed close to Ashlyn's side.

Thank God for him.

I wish I could offer him free drinks for the rest of the night—a small token of gratitude. But that would give me away, and I can't afford to do that.

I'm probably being a total asshole anyway.

What if Ashlyn really likes Mr. Tall? I can't stand in the way of that. I have no rights at all when it comes to my childhood crush.

Crush.

Love.

Shit, I ruined it.

When I left that night, I never really thought through everything I was running away from. I've lived with years of regret ever since. But it's too late now. I made my choices, and now I have to live with the consequences.

12

A CHANCE FOR CLOSURE

Ashlyn

THE FIRST THING TO wake me is the sound of an engine.

My forehead wrinkles, and I stretch a hand over my head, trying to identify the noise. I didn't think there were vehicles on this island. Rolling over, I sit up on my elbow, and then a snicker pops out of me—soft and breathy— when I realize it's actually Leo snoring.

Tipping my head, I eye my friend with affection. He's still in his pink shirt, which has ridden up to reveal the bottom of his slightly rounded belly. His naked legs are sprawled over the duvet cover like a starfish. Thank goodness he kept his underwear on!

Biting my lower lip, I give him an adoring grin before

easing out of bed. By the time we got back to our bungalow last night, I was still sober enough to change into boxer shorts and a tank top. Leo… well, he was a little more wasted than me.

There's a minor dull ache between my eyes, and I wash my face and down a glass of water, trying to eradicate the feeling. I could have gotten as drunk as my bestie, but I kind of wanted to keep my wits about me. Varam was getting handsier by the hour, his dancing sloppy and unco-ordinated. It was a relief to use Leo as my excuse to call it quits for the night.

The bar had already closed when I helped Leo stagger to bed. I didn't see Cooper again, but that didn't stop me from dreaming about him.

Gazing into the mirror, I catch the water dripping off my chin before drying my face and tying my hair into a messy bun. Long tendrils of unkempt waves frame my cheeks. I run a finger under my eyes and decide not to worry with makeup. It's still early and it'd be nice to walk on the beach before breakfast. Most people will still be sleeping, and I can spend a little time with the beautiful sunrise and peaceful ocean.

Throwing on my bikini and a light summer dress, I slip out the sliding glass door and take in the apricot sky.

Wow. So stunning.

For a moment, it reminds me of the vast sky in Montana. The colors created behind those mountains were breathtaking.

You should call Cooper's brothers. Let them know he's here.

I'm surprised the thought didn't hit me earlier. It probably should have been one of my first, but I guess I was recovering from the shock of seeing Cooper again... and the disappointment of him not acknowledging me.

It's him. Deep down I *know* it is, but I don't feel right about calling his brothers until I have actual confirmation.

Besides, what if Cooper doesn't want to be found?

He obviously disappeared for a reason, and stayed hidden as well.

The idea of him shacked up with an island girl bothers me, but I try to shake it off and think logically.

He's miles from home, living on a little island with no cell phone coverage and groups that max out around 40. Rich, luxurious people who are so far removed from his past that they'd never be able to make a connection. This is a perfect hiding place for him.

It must have thrown him so completely to see me yesterday.

Walking down the cobbled path, I duck around a massive hibiscus plant and find the steps leading down to the sand. It's cold beneath my toes, and I smile at the sensation, my heart finding solace in the gentle lap of the ocean.

I head for the water, dipping my toes into it before standing to drink in the vast ocean and pale orange sky. As the sun rises, these colors will morph into a brilliant blue.

Yeah, it's going to be a stunning day.

"Hey, Ash." Paul puffs past me, raising his hand in greeting.

I wave at him and Harry as they stride down the beach.

The fitness junkies can't miss a run and workout, not even on vacation.

I shake my head, amused at their drive. I don't know if I've ever been that motivated over anything before. I'm one of those "happy just to cruise through life" people. At least I thought I was. That niggle in my chest tells me I might be wrong about that, but I'm just not sure.

I wander the shoreline, watching the sky lighten and letting the gentle breeze play with the tendrils of hair around my face. They tickle and dance, but I let them, a soft melancholy I can't explain riding through me.

Stopping at the end of the cove, I drink in the view and inhale the cool morning air.

Christmas is tomorrow.

Feels weird not being wrapped up in a big jacket and scrunching my shoulders as I bustle through snowy New York streets. Shopping bags would be crammed on each arm as I tried to cater to my friends and family.

But not this year. We all agreed not to give each other presents. It would've been too hard to cart them all here. We're going to get together in the new year and have a massive present party—play that game where you each bring a mystery gift and then take turns unwrapping a box or stealing a gift off someone else. It'll be fun. It's nice to do something different, and way less pressure.

Yes. The island definitely nurtures that need to just slow down and enjoy the moment.

With another deep breath and a little nod, I head back to the resort. Leo might still be asleep, but Shira will probably wake soon, and we can share a breakfast smoothie or something while we wait for him.

I head up the first set of stairs I find and come across the large pool area that I didn't get to explore yesterday. It's impressive, the waterfall dropping into a wide rectangular pool that then curves around the corner to the front entrance and jetty. I spy the covered bar at the end and track to the bridge where I can cross directly into the restaurant. Down from that area is a line of neatly laid out deck chairs, and look, there's Cooper cleaning the pool.

I jerk, my heart suddenly taking off like I just heard a gunshot behind me.

Crossing my arms, I stare at him for a moment, wondering what to do.

I could simply ignore him, cross the bridge and head back to my bungalow via the restaurant.

Or I could not.

I could turn and wander around the edge of the pool, taking my time to get to the front entrance and brushing right past Cooper on the way.

Should I do it?

He turns and spots me, jolting a little before finding his composure. I wonder if he sees the indecision on my face.

He's still looking at me, gripping the rod of the pool-cleaning tool like he's forgotten how to use it. I watch his knuckles whiten, then relax, whiten, then relax.

We're trapped in a silent stare, just like we were in the bathroom yesterday.

He knows me.

He remembers who I am.

But he doesn't want to.

Ouch. That really hurts.

I should just cross the bridge.

And let it plague you for the rest of the day? You're going to be bumping into him again! Just deal with it.

My nose scrunches as my body takes over and pulls me toward him.

Closure.

Yeah, that's what I'll tell myself. I need closure. I haven't had it all this time and maybe that's why I couldn't let go.

I'll walk up, tell him who I am, and then we can be done with it.

Closure.

With a thick swallow, I approach. He steps sideways, like I'm infected with the plague, and looks to the pool, his movements quick and erratic as he starts cleaning with a new fervor.

With a serene smile, I politely greet him. "Morning."

"Good morning," he murmurs.

Great. How do I start this?

"Uh… looks like it's going to be a nice day."

Ugh. The weather? Seriously? That's so awkward!

Cooper glances over his shoulder, staring out at the ocean. "Yeah, kind of perfect, actually. The weather report was good when I checked it this morning. High of 78, a nice offshore breeze, clear skies for most of the day."

Oh, his voice.

It's deep and husky, maybe a little more raw than it used to be.

I remember the summer it changed. Those odd squeaks and cracks as his voice broke and then became that spine-tingling, heart-racing, stomach-thrilling sound that would skitter over my body and make me all warm and goocy at the same time.

I've missed him so much!

My voice quakes a little as I try to play it cool. "Nice. So... will you be taking a tour out on the water?"

He hesitates and then nods, like he's reluctant to admit it. "Yep. I'm the snorkel guy this morning."

Right, so now I have to go snorkeling.

No you don't!

Ah, yeah, I do!

I gaze at him again, letting my eyes trail over his body. It's impossible not to admire the view. He's bigger than he used to be, but in all the right ways. His muscles look harder, stronger, and more tanned than before. I used to know the shape of them so well. Would they still feel the same beneath my fingers?

Without meaning to, I rub my thumb over my fingertips and wonder.

He clears his throat, like my perusal is making him uncomfortable.

I jerk straight, heat flashing through me.

Yeah, I should go. Just walk back to my bungalow and hide under the covers for the rest of the day.

You'll regret that!

I go to move past him, then force myself to stop.

Do it! Just say it!

With a short huff, I flick a wave of hair off my cheek and blurt, "You don't remember me, do you, Cooper Barrett?"

He goes still but doesn't say anything. His thumb picks at the blue plastic handle, and yeah, I'm pretty sure humiliation is about to set in big-time.

I should have just kept my mouth shut.

13

THE CHOICE IS PAIN OR PAIN

Cooper

MY HEART IS THUNDERING.

That one little question should be as simple as, "Yeah, of course I do."

But it's not.

It's loaded with so much meaning, because it has to be.

I don't just remember her; it's like I'm breathing her all over again, and how I answer is so vitally important.

"Nope! I'm pretty sure we've never met."

Just say that. One little lie and she'll walk away. This will be over.

I force my gaze up from the pool water, and it's the biggest mistake I could have made.

She's looking right at me. Those green eyes of hers, that soft, hopeful smile.

I dreamed about it all freaking night.

And now she's standing in front of me in a see-through summer dress that's catching the light and showing me the soft pink bikini underneath. It fits her perfectly, wrapping around delicate curves and making my head spin.

She was always beautiful, even as a twelve-year-old, but now she's something else.

There's no more girl left in her. She's all woman.

A freaking supermodel woman who is making my knees want to buckle. If I drop to the tiles around the pool and beg her to forgive me, would she do it?

You can't do that!

You left for a good reason, remember? You don't deserve her! Just concentrate on cleaning the frickin' pool!

I grip the vacuum I'm using to catch stray debris that falls into the pool overnight, but I can't move it. I'm just standing there like an idiot, not moving and not saying anything.

"You were my first kiss." Her voice is whisper-soft, light with nostalgia. It matches the pale blush on her cheeks. She's not wearing any makeup right now, so I can see it all so clearly.

My entire body sparks with memories that turn into fantasies. What if I dropped this damn pool cleaner right now and took her face in my hands? What if I cupped the back of her head and planted my lips on hers? My tongue would seek hers out, finding that delectable warmth so easily. It'd be like going home.

My muscles are practically vibrating with desire.

There's been no one since her.

Not even a kiss.

That may sound lame, but no woman has captured me. Many have definitely tried, but I just wasn't interested. Cheap thrills and instant highs couldn't relieve the ache in my chest. I only ever wanted deep and meaningful. And I had it with Ashlyn.

She's the one.

And I so wish I could tell her.

But even if I wanted to, I couldn't.

My tongue is concrete—set and immobile.

Her smile starts to falter, her green eyes scrunching with disappointment. "Maybe I've got it wrong. Or maybe you just don't remember me. Or you've moved on and you shouldn't be talking to me because you have a girlfriend or a wife or…"

Her voice trails off, but she keeps staring at my face, like the idea of me being with someone else is painful for her. Her eyes are begging me to deny it, because she can't give up hope just yet.

My head shakes before I can stop it. "No girlfriend. No wife."

What are you doing? Shut up! Shut up right now!

I just can't stand the idea of her thinking I'm with someone else.

Why? Wouldn't that be easier?

Walk. Away! Stop what you're doing and walk away!

What kind of asshole does that?

I can't do that to her.

But I can't give her false hope either.

So, what do I say?

"Yeah, I remember you, but please don't talk to me again. I'm no good for you. We can't ever be what we were."

Pain. Pain. Pain.

That's all my words will cause.

But my silence is causing it too.

I can't win!

"I'm not…" I sigh. Looking away from her, I study the ocean, the salty breeze hitting my dry lips. I wish it held some kind of magic cure for my chaotic brain.

Give me the words I need, ocean breeze. Tell me what to do!

I lick my lips, but the plea is a futile one.

After a long, uncomfortable beat, Ashlyn clears her throat and dips her chin. Her smile is sad as she runs a hand down her bare arm before holding her elbow.

Yeah, she knows how stubborn I can be. If I don't want to talk, I won't. My "I'm not…" is all she's going to get.

"Sorry for bothering you," she murmurs, moving around me.

A sweet smell of lilac follows in her wake. She must still use the same shampoo.

It revives memories, stirs the flame she ignited the second she stepped into the bathroom yesterday.

I don't dare reach for her, but watching her walk away is killing me. The breeze catches her long hair, making it dance across her back. I still remember the feel of those tendrils between my fingers, the sweet tang of her lips, the melody of her laughter against my cheek.

It calls to me like a siren, and before she can get any farther away, I forget every inhibition and admit the truth. "I do remember you, Smoky."

14

A KISS THAT WAS MEANT TO BE

I STOP MID-STEP, resting my big toe on the hard tile beneath me and pivoting to face him.

It's hard to breathe, the air in my lungs is too thin, the dancing fairies in my stomach too erratic.

What did he just call me?

Smoky.

I can't believe it.

He called me Smoky.

As a smile starts to curl the edges of my mouth, my mind takes me back in time to a hot summer's day in a shaded wood near the Barrett ranch.

"Oh, because my name's Ashlyn? Ash? That's why you call me Smoky, right?" I gave him a playful scowl and shook my head. "You know it's not that funny."

He laughed, the sound just starting to deepen with his age. Leaning against the pine tree trunk, he crossed his arms and gazed at me. "I don't call you Smoky because of your name."

"Then why do you?" I narrowed my eyes at him, pinching my thumb behind my back and trying to look cross when I really didn't feel anything like that at all.

The butterflies in my belly were chaotic, my temperature spiking as I tried to rein in my delight and play this game with him. His hazel eyes were light and playful, but there was something else in his gaze that made my toes tingle and my heart stutter.

What's he going to say to me?

Why Smoky?

His swallow was loud, a sweet look of vulnerability flashing over his expression when he whispered, "It's because you're so hot." His shoulder hitched like the confession was no big deal.

But it was! It was!

"You know, smokin' hot. Like…" He swallowed the last word, but I was pretty sure he said sexy.

Oh my gosh!

Cooper thinks I'm sexy.

It was an effort not to whoop and jump into the air.

That was what my butterflies wanted me to do. Anything to release the pent-up joy trilling through me.

We'd known each other for a couple years and had been sneaking away to hang out any chance we could. My crush started by the end of Summer One, but I'd had my doubts that it'd ever be reciprocated. Cooper was pretty good at keeping things close to his chest.

But Summer Three had been a little different.

Maybe it was because I was fourteen and my boobs were really starting to come in.

Or maybe it was because he was turning from boy to man.

I didn't know, but the underlying chemistry between us had been intense.

So maybe it was time to act on it.

Dancing over the dry needles, I nestled my hands in the back pockets of my frayed denim shorts and approached him. "You wanna kiss me?"

It was the scariest question I'd ever asked a person, and I waited in agony while he took his sweet time to respond.

"Yeah," he rasped and then swallowed again.

I bit my lip, trying to control my smile, but it was no use. "I've never kissed a guy before."

"Me neither."

His joke made me giggle, and I took another step closer. We were one step away from touching. If I leaned in, I'd be able to feel his breath on my skin. "Have you ever kissed a girl?"

He studied my face for a long minute, gently tucking

the hair behind my shoulder. "Only in my imagination. I've kissed you a hundred times in my mind."

I took that final step, resting my hands lightly on his chest before leaning toward his mouth. I stopped an inch from his lips, my voice trembling just a little. "I hope the reality's better."

"It will be."

And then his lips pressed against mine. We both seemed a little tentative at first, but it felt incredible. His mouth was soft and sweet, the sensation a heady rush.

We were kissing!

My first kiss!

My stomach started to shake as I leaned a little closer against him. His hand shimmied down my back, then came to rest on my waist, then my hip, then my waist again. I understood the indecision, because I didn't know what to do with my hands either.

Put them in his hair. Or on his neck or something. That's what they do in the movies!

I lightly placed my fingers on his neck, trailing them over his skin and up into the short blades of hair behind his ears.

I wondered what would happen next.

Did I open my mouth?

Was that too forward?

I—

Cooper pulled back, his hazel gaze drinking me in. It was a look I'd never seen before—wonder, joy, amazement. It made me feel pretty damn special and I smiled, trying to think of something cool to say.

But Cooper beat me to it.

"Yeah, it's definitely better." His words came out in a rushed whisper, and then he was diving for my mouth again. Our lips met with a new confidence, our mouths opening like something else was taking charge and leading the way.

Maybe it was our souls.

I didn't know, but whatever was causing that heady explosion could take me anywhere it wanted to.

My tongue was born to dance with Cooper's. My body wanted to explore every taste sensation, feel every vibration and sizzle that ran throughout my body.

Just like Cooper, I'd imagined the moment, that first kiss. I'd wistfully lain in my bed dreaming about it, dying for the summer to come a little faster, just so I could see him again.

And it was happening.

Our first kiss.

It wasn't awkward, it was epic.

It was meant to be.

15

SUCH A GONER

Cooper

"THAT WAS ONE HELL OF A KISS," I murmur, bright memories fading as I force them away from me.

Ashlyn's sweet taste lingered for the rest of that day, fueling an appetite I didn't even realize I had. I mean, I knew I liked her, but after that kiss, I hungered for any second I could spend with her.

She became my biggest, most important reason to live.

That was the greatest summer.

Or maybe it was the one after that, when she returned, that much older and prettier, that much more familiar. Every summer brought something fresh and new with it. Something delectable and precious.

"They all were." Her soft words and magnificent smile plunge me back into reality, and I'm powerless against her flirtatious look.

I nearly reach for her.

Nearly forget my place, my reasoning, the past five years of hell.

But a loud laugh from the restaurant snaps me to attention.

Fear spikes through me, like a javelin's been shoved through the back of my neck.

Shit, I want to tell her everything and nothing. I want to admit it all and run the other direction so I never have to explain.

Frozen in this point of indecision, I stare at her, not even knowing what my face is doing.

Her smile slips, concern wrinkling her forehead as she reaches for me.

No, she can't touch you! You'll never recover!

I take a step back, and the pained look on her face is a blade through my stomach.

How do I explain this to her?

I can't. I—

"Ashlyn!" I'm saved by Mr. Tall.

He appears around the corner, a broad smile taking over his face when he spots her.

"Hey!" He raises his hand and jogs around the restaurant. "I've been looking for you."

Ashlyn glances at me, her nose wrinkling like that's the last thing she wants, but she pastes on a smile and turns to face him. "Morning, Varam."

"You're looking beautiful." He eyes her the way he did last night, and I grip the pool cleaner, the plastic ribbing on the handle digging into my palm.

"Thank you." Her words are clipped and polite.

She's making it abundantly clear that she doesn't need compliments like that from him, but Varam is oblivious.

Part of me wants to step between them so she doesn't have to deal with this idiot, but it's not my place.

Dammit!

Dammit!

It should be my place!

Why did I leave her?

You know why. Now shut up and get back to cleaning the pool!

Ashlyn glances at me again, but I avoid her gaze this time, focusing on my job. This pool is going to be so freaking clean by the time I'm done!

I refuse to look at her again, even though it causes this sharp pain in my stomach and chest. It's weird how emotion can sometimes be physical. But it can. I ached all over when I first left my brothers. Those months following Grandpa's death made my head pound. Stomaching food was nearly impossible. I wanted to waste away to nothing, yet instinct kept me eating, forced me to find work, to live each day in spite of the fact that I wanted to curl into a ball and join my mother.

She was probably in heaven, though… along with Grandpa.

Not me. I knew exactly where I'd be going when I breathed my last, and maybe that was why I kept on living.

"Want to have some breakfast with me?" Varam tries to slide his hand down Ashlyn's back, but she subtly moves out of reach. A slight frown crinkles his expression, but he slips his hand into his pocket like that was his intention all along. "The buffet looks amazing."

"Uh… yeah, um… are Shira and Lance—"

Ashlyn doesn't get time to finish her sentence because two more of her friends appear. I can feel her relief like a palpable vibe that travels from her to me.

Are we still connected?

Could we still do that thing where we could talk without words?

I'm too afraid to find out, so I keep my eyes on the water below me.

"Hey, beautiful!" Shira lifts her phone and snaps a pic, then giggles and does a selfie with her man before taking a few more shots of the morning beach. "This place is so freaking gorgeous! I want to live here forever."

Lance laughs and kisses her bare shoulder. "Come on, baby. Let's go have some breakfast."

"Excellent, I'm starving." She looks to Ashlyn, then around, before frowning. "Where's Leo?"

"Dead to the world when I left him." Ashlyn walks away from me, not looking back.

That's good.

So why does it hurt, then?

"And no doubt snoring like a freight train." Shira cracks up laughing while Lance chimes in.

"I don't know how you share a room with that guy."

"He's my best friend."

"And you don't have a boyfriend, I guess."

Varam jumps all over that one. "You're welcome to bunk with me."

I tense, fisting my hand and resisting the urge to punch something. Scowling at the guy's back, I keep my eyes narrowed on the crown of his head, pleased when Ashlyn moves away from him so she can stand on the other side of Shira.

They travel away in a high-speed talking group.

Ashlyn glances back once to look at me, but I keep my eyes down.

I feel like I spent the rest of the morning that way, studying the tiles, the sand, the concrete beneath me.

But then comes that moment where I have to look up and face the world again.

All my morning jobs are done, I've had my breakfast and organized the snorkeling gear. Now I'm waiting on the water's edge, ready to load up the island's boat with enthusiastic guests.

And there she is again, walking right for me like a vision.

There's no sundress anymore, just a red-hot bikini that fits over her breasts perfectly.

And her legs. Oh God, her legs.

Did they get longer over the last few years?

They definitely got more toned, more luscious.

Her hips sway a little as she drapes a towel over her shoulder and laughs at something Leo said. It's not a conscious "look at me" action, just a subtle move of the body that's hypnotizing.

I am such a goner.

Who the hell am I kidding thinking I can just let this woman go?

16

ONE SEA TURTLE AND AN
AWKWARD CONVERSATION

Ashlyn

THE BOAT IS SIMPLE—WHITE with *Paradis Idyllique* written in calligraphy on the side. We wade into the water and climb the small stepladder, finding our seats amongst the snorkeling gear piled at our feet.

I get as close to the steering wheel as possible, taking the seat right near the end of the bench, so I can watch Cooper in his board shorts that seem to magically perch on his hips without falling. I study the shape of his toned torso and tanned skin as he instructs us about boat safety and then starts the engine.

My shades hide my ogling, but I wonder if Cooper can

still feel my perusal anyway. He's wearing sunglasses too, so I can't really tell.

But he remembers me.

Smoky.

That'll carry me through the rest of the day. I mean, make me freaking *fly* through the rest of the day.

Remembering our first kiss filled me with love bubbles all over again. Who knew they were just below the surface all that time? And it barely took a scratch to unearth them all again.

My stomach jitters so hard I wonder if I'm sick from love or the bouncing boat. The ride is a rocky one as we chop over waves and out to a quiet spot about a mile from the island. Apparently it's great for snorkeling.

Leo and Lance are trying to have a yelled conversation above the roar of the boat engine, but I tune it out, pretending to look at the water while giving my peripheral vision a thorough workout. I love the way the muscles in Cooper's arms flex. It's just a subtle shift, but it makes his forearms sexy. Who knew forearms could be sexy? I like his chunky watch and those braided leather bracelets piled above them. Who gifted them to him? Or did he make them himself?

I really want to find a time to talk to Cooper again. I want answers to all my questions, both big and small. This morning was cut short thanks to Varam, who is sitting across from me and openly staring like he's never seen a bikini before.

Ugh. I am absolutely swimming away from this guy when we jump off the boat.

I picture myself slicing through the water, kicking my flippers hard to get some distance and then focusing on fish so I can have a chance to figure out what to do.

I have to speak to Cooper again.

I have to tell him about his brothers.

But will that just push him away?

I'm desperate for every detail of why he left and where the hell he's been, but I don't know how to begin a conversation like that. The hurt of his departure lingers beneath the bubbles of joy, and I really should process that, but it's so heavy. Cooper spoke to me! He acknowledged our past, and I want to build on that, not make him run away again.

Maybe it's best if I keep things light and playful to start with. Act like my heart was never broken and it's just really great to see him looking so good and healthy. You know, just like old high school buddies who bump into each other on the street—laughter, a few "had to be there" jokes. Good times!

Can I pull that off?

Can Cooper?

My nose wrinkles as I try to picture the scene in my head, but I run out of time, because the boat slows and we're soon bobbing in the water.

"Okay, guys. This is it." Cooper claps his hands together, giving them a little rub before launching into safety guidelines. We sit through the dos and don'ts. I pray my friends are paying attention. This bunch can get a little crazy, and I really don't want them to embarrass me in front of Cooper. He'll wonder what I'm doing hanging out with this crowd, and I'll have to say… "I'm not actually sure."

I mean, Leo and Shira are easy answers, and I guess Lance kind of comes with that too. I'll never lose touch with them. But the other "friends" I've been hanging with… is it sad that I could kind of take or leave them?

Oh man, that makes me sound like such an awful person!

Shame on me.

I push the shades back up my nose and nod at Cooper's last instruction, then reach for the snorkeling gear. It doesn't take long to get suited up. Sitting on the side, I swing my awkward flipper feet around, hold my nose and jump into the water.

It's cool and refreshing—the perfect temperature. It feels so good on my skin and I tread water for a few minutes, basking in the warmth of the sun on my face and the weightless joy of being in the ocean.

The flippers on my feet feel heavy and foreign, but I pump my legs a little harder and get used to it.

Once Leo and Shira are ready to go, we follow Paul and Hugh, who are already searching for fish, their snorkels above the water while their heads are ducked below. Mel and Teagan are laughing and squealing over something. Cooper swims their direction to no doubt check they're okay.

Man, he's got a nice style.

So smooth and masculine, like he was born half merman.

"Mm-hmm. He's a hottie all right. Damn, girl." Leo

shakes his snorkel face at me, and I giggle. He looks hilarious right now, his round face compressed by the mask, his voice kind of nasally.

I haven't had a chance to tell him I talked to Cooper this morning. Shira peppered me with questions at the buffet line, but I told her to zip it. Varam and Lance were right there, and I don't want them knowing.

She was well behaved after that, but I know she'll snag me at some point and demand all the details.

Am I ready to give them to her?

Of course you are! She's your best friend!

I shut the thought off and put the snorkel mouthpiece between my lips. Biting on the plastic, I try out a couple breaths, then turn to my stomach and start exploring the ocean floor.

It's freaking beautiful!

A kaleidoscope of colors zigzag below me. Zebra fish, yellow fish with black stripes, bright orange starfish. Oh my gosh, there's a sea turtle!

I kick after it, gliding through the clear water, marveling at the way the sunlight plays and shimmers below the surface. The turtle's fins pump back and I kick a little harder, wanting a closer look.

Its hard brown shell is patterned like a jigsaw puzzle. I study the lines, getting over top of him while still keeping a respectable distance. I don't want to scare the poor guy.

He's so cool, and his little face! Adorable!

Hey, dude!

I laugh in my head, thinking of *Finding Nemo* and the cool surfy sea turtles.

I wonder where his buddies are... and if it's even a he. Maybe it's a she turtle.

Enraptured by the creature, I follow it until it pumps its fins a little harder and obviously wants to get away from me.

I slow and let him go, then rise to the surface to get my bearings again.

My head pops out of the water and I do a spin, looking for my buddies. I can't see them nearby and for a second wonder where the hell everyone is.

Ripping off my mask, I wipe my eyes for a better view and nearly jump out of my skin when a deep voice behind me says, "This way."

I spin with a gasp, then tip my head back, letting out a laugh to the sky. "You scared me."

"Sorry." Cooper perches his mask on top of his head and gives me an impish grin.

So familiar.

I always loved that expression on him.

"You were swimming a little far out, so I thought I better follow you." He points to his left, and I see my friends in the distance. "Can't lose one of my group."

"Of course." I swim closer to him, and we tread water face-to-face. Neither of us seems that keen to go back, so I take advantage of the moment.

Light. Playful.

"I was following a sea turtle." I grin.

"Oh yeah?" His smile matches mine, and it does things to my heart. "Those things are pretty cool. I've ridden one of the big ones before. Well, you know, kind of. He let me hold his shell for a bit."

"That is so cool!" My voice pitches with excitement. "Man, you must love living here."

He nods, his smile faltering for a moment. "It's a beautiful place. Anything in nature suits me just fine."

He always did love the outdoors. He seemed to have this innate intuition when it came to the woods and animals. His brothers always joked that the cattle loved him and Michael the most. They just seemed to have a way with animals.

"Born for the land." He told me his grandpa said that to him. Man, he was so proud about that. He loved the ranch more than anything. It was his haven.

I should tell him that his family is back there.

Say it! Just say it!

My lips part, the words jamming in my throat as I watch the water droplets glide down Cooper's face and into his beard.

He was eighteen when he left, already a man in some ways, but there's something more mature about him now. More wounded.

Oh my gosh, so much emotion right now.

"It's good to see you again." The words come out rusty and uneven, like I'm speaking with laryngitis.

He blinks and swallows. The light and playful I was going for just disintegrated.

With a pained frown, he nods, then tips his head to the right—a silent "we should get back."

Putting his mask on, he ducks below the water, kicking his flippers and speeding off like a torpedo.

I follow him, my deflated spirit struggling to keep up with him.

I half-heartedly kick my legs, returning to my rambunctious friends and pasting on a smile when I resurface and listen to Leo's enthusiastic story about a school of zebra fish.

Doing my best to focus on his every word, I try to distract myself from the popped balloon in my chest. Reaching Cooper is going to be harder than I thought.

If he doesn't appreciate a simple "It's nice to see you again," how's he going to cope with "Your brothers are back and they want you home"?

Is it really my duty to be the person to tell him?

If you don't say it, who will?

You could just tell his brothers he's here, and they could come get him.

Or you could get over yourself and find some courage!

I close my eyes against my warring brain.

"Ash, you okay?" Leo stops his story mid-sentence.

My eyes pop open, and I paste on a smile. "Yeah, of course."

"Well, put that mask back on and let me show you, then!"

As soon as I do as he says, he grabs my hand and forces me below the water, pointing and waving, then giving me a thumbs up.

Varam swims over with his underwater camera, and

we pose for some pics. I'm grateful for my mask because smiling right now is an effort.

All I want is to take Cooper's hand and find an isolated spot on the island. A place we can talk and reconnect without anyone interrupting us.

Man, that would be fantastic.

If only he'd let me do it.

17

THUNDERSTRUCK

Cooper

"IT'S *nice to see you too.*"

How hard would that have been to say?

But no, I had to go and make things awkward by getting quiet and morose. Killing Ashlyn's dazzling smile with a little head nod and subject change.

You're a freaking idiot!

I'm torn between wanting to get the hell off this island and wanting to spend every second I can with her.

I *should* want to disappear, which is why when Bembe asked me to swap and take a group hiking this afternoon, I should have said no. But I agreed, because that's what I do, and now she's five steps behind me and wearing frayed denim shorts.

Of all things.

They're just like the ones she used to wear, but again, somehow sexier.

This is torture.

A new, delicious kind of torture.

Squeezing my eyes shut, I pinch the bridge of my nose, then push my shades back up.

We're hiking to the small waterfall this afternoon. It's about a thirty-minute trek from the resort down a jungle-lined pathway that echoes with birds squawking and singing to each other. Colors pop, tourists "Ahh" and snap photographs. It's an idyllic slice of utopia that we work hard to maintain and keep beautiful.

The sun is past its midday high, and the heat is just perfect for a dip in the oasis I'm taking them to. By the time we get there, we'll all be hot and sweaty. Cooling off in the water and experiencing that rush of jumping off the short waterfall will be just what everyone needs.

I think of the group I took up there last month and can't help a small grin. Five families were staying on the island together, and there was a bunch of overactive teenage boys who were out to impress the ladies. They flipped and dived off that rock like their lives depended on it.

Such showmen.

It took me back in time, and I turned them into my brothers. Brody and Deeks would have been showing off while Jake did a thorough mental analysis, working out how safe everything would be before giving it a try. Michael would have stood back until everyone had strutted their stuff, then humbly pulled off a move that would make us all gape.

I miss my brothers.

Clearing my throat, I shut the thought off before it can grow. I don't want to picture what they're doing right now, or worse, think about what I put them through when I left.

Guilt singes, burns, annihilates.

Trying to convince myself that I did the right thing is easier some days than others. If I'm purely logical about it, I did the right thing. Raise four kids on my own? I was eighteen! I couldn't run a ranch and take responsibility for my brothers without Grandpa to help me. I was out of my depth, not to mention the fact that I'd—

Snapping the memory off, I try to avoid the emotion that roars through me. It's a cruel beast that says the opposite to logic, taunts me in my sleep, batters me when my guard's down and reminds me that I abandoned the people I love the most in this world.

"Hey." A perky girl with a swishing ponytail bobs past me. "Mind if we go ahead?"

I glance at the guy holding her hand and make a quick judgment call. "Sure. We won't be far behind you. Just stay on the path and look out for the wooden sign. It'll be about knee height and has a left arrow pointing to the waterhole."

"Sounds good. Thanks." She pulls her guy ahead and giggles.

I'm so busy watching them go that I don't even notice Ashlyn until she's right beside me. I flinch but force myself to play it cool and not let my stride falter.

I watch her from the corner of my eye, my forehead creasing with a frown.

Her expression is tight with obvious frustration. "Mind if I walk with you for a minute?"

"Sure." I glance over my shoulder and spot the guy I figured would be there. Mr. Tall. Varam, I think she called him this morning. My eyes graze the rest of the party behind us before I turn back to her.

It's weird. These people don't seem like Ashlyn's crew.

Not that I ever knew her outside of Montana, but she never struck me as one of those rich glamor girls, yet she's surrounded by them. They're definitely not like the down-to-earth friends she used to tell me about. The ones who climbed trees to throw snowballs on the bullies' heads or dared each other to eat a cheeseburger in less than four bites.

The stories she used to tell always made me laugh. She was so bright and expressive when she talked, her eyes like dancing fireflies, her words like a happy robin's song.

I guess people change. You grow up, get more serious as adulting has to find a place in your life.

I'm not the guy I was when we spent our summers together.

It's weird how sad that suddenly makes me.

Ashlyn's not saying anything, her lips set in a thin line, her delicate nostrils flaring when she shakes her head.

"Tall Guy getting too much for you, huh?"

"He just doesn't listen," she snaps, then lowers her voice. "He's spent his whole life having people serve him and give him everything he wants. He can't comprehend that I wouldn't be interested in his wealth and influence. No matter how many times I try to kindly say I'm not looking for a relationship, he just keeps on trying. It's like I'm this challenge he has to win."

My eyebrows dip into another frown, and I turn to check on where the guy is. Thankfully he's talking to another tall guy and looks pretty wrapped up in the conversation.

"So, wealthy and powerful's not your type, huh?"

"No." She raises her eyebrows, her tone emphatic.

The pointed look on her face makes me grin, and I engage before I can stop myself. "What type of guys do you usually go for, then?"

The edge of her mouth curls up as she throws me a sideways glance. "You trying to ask about my dating history?"

I wince and scratch the back of my neck. "I probably shouldn't."

She scoffs and shakes her head. "It's been dismal. I've had the odd relationship, but nothing that's lasted more than a month or two."

I pause when we reach the sign, kind of happy about her admission. Which is so bad! I should *want* for her to fall in love and be happy. What is wrong with me?

She turns the direction I'm pointing, and just as we reach the waterhole, she spins back and looks me square in the eye.

"I guess I never got over my first crush. He was something… spectacular." Her voice matches the dreamy smile she's shining all over me. "No one else can compare." She takes my breath away with a heartfelt grin, then winks as Leo brushes past her and starts gushing.

"Oh my gosh! Beautiful! I am moving here. This is my new home!" Leo's voice rises like a pop song, racing down through the group.

They all rush forward to take in the picture-perfect swimming hole. The water is churned white by the little waterfall cascading between the rocks. The luscious trees bursting along the edge are like natural umbrellas, and no matter who comes here, they always have the same reaction.

"Holy shit. This place is amazing!"

"Unbelievable."

"So gorgeous."

The gasping, oohing, and aahing usually makes me smile, but I'm still thunderstruck by what Ashlyn just said. Her brazen flirting has twisted my heart out of shape. It's struggling to beat normally, and my lungs suddenly feel full of helium. If I speak right now, I'm going to sound like a moron, I'm sure of it.

"Thank you. Thank you." Leo pats my chest, then kisses my cheek, letting out another sound of joy as he jumps past me to go and stand with Ashlyn.

She's gazing into the oasis with a whisper of a smile, drinking in the natural beauty and so obviously trying not to look at me.

I can't believe she just said that.

No other relationships since me? Well, none that really counted.

How can that be?

She's such a catch. Any guy would be lucky to have her.

You've never moved on with another girl. Maybe you took her heart, just like she took yours. Is that really so hard to believe?

No. It's not.

That's the scary part.

She's making it nearly impossible to stick to my resolve. It's weakening by the hour, and as much as I should fight it, I'm wondering if it'll just be a losing battle.

So why not give in and let my heart win for a change?

18

WANT VIBES AND FIREWORKS

SO I SAID IT. I just blurted it out loud, and now I can't look at Cooper.

I feel like I'm thirteen all over again and realizing I have a huge crush on my summer friend and not knowing what to do about it.

I guess I never got over my first crush.

Ugh! I didn't!

What the hell am I trying to achieve right now?

Do I want to pick things up where they left off?

Cooper abandoned his family... and me! He hasn't been in touch, so obviously he wants to be away from the old life he had. Why would he want me now?

But the way he looked at me when I walked toward the boat this morning. The way his gaze lingered when I joined the hiking group this afternoon...

I'm sensing mega "want" vibes, but that doesn't mean he's going to act on them.

Cooper's one of the most disciplined, self-contained people I know. I'll only break through his barrier if he wants me to.

"I'm jumping off the waterfall!" Shira springs between Leo and me. "Lance just dared me to."

With an excited squeal, she follows her boyfriend around the rocks, heading for the waterfall. Cooper gave us the rundown before we left on the hike, saying we were free to jump if we wanted to, then warned us of the dangers.

I see him moving, his eyes tracking the people who are climbing up to attempt the somewhat daring move. It's no doubt totally safe, but it looks a little scary to me, so I linger back... until Leo shrugs.

"What the hell, let's do it."

Taking my hand, he tries to drag me.

"I don't think so."

"Why not?" Pulling his shades off, he dumps them on top of our towels and pouts at me. "You gotta come with me."

I make a face, shaking my head.

"He wouldn't have said we could do it if it wasn't safe. Don't be a 'fraidy cat. Come on, girl."

"You go ahead. Let me just... watch you do it one time and then I might."

With an exaggerated eye roll, Leo heads for the rocks, climbing over and around the back to pop up behind Shira and Lance.

My best friend squeals, waving at me, before her fiancé pulls her in for a passionate kiss. The crowd hollers and whoops; then Lance takes her hand and they jump into the water together.

I clap with everybody else when they resurface, then stand back and watch while basically everyone else has a go.

Varam does a showy flip that gets an extra loud cheer. He surfaces and looks straight at me, flicking black hair off his face and throwing me a dazzling smile. "Come on, Ashlyn! You have to jump too!"

"Jump! Jump! Jump!" they all start chanting.

Dammit! Talk about pressure.

I give them a tight smile and try to laugh it off, but they just won't quit. Not until I flick my hands at them and shout, "Okay, fine!"

Cheers rise from the water as I shed my jean shorts, then cross my arms and reluctantly make my way to the rocks.

Leo's still in the water, so I guess we won't be jumping together.

Crap, everyone will be watching. That's why I've left my tank top on. I don't care if it gets wet, I don't want my bikini top shooting up so everyone can see the goodies. Talk about humiliating!

I get to the base of the trail that leads up to the

jumping point. I can hear the water rushing above me and chew my lip.

"You okay?" Cooper's voice is soft and sweet, just the way I remember it.

I turn, my smile small, tentative. "Just don't want to get wet, really."

That is such a lie, and he knows it.

I wince, settling on the truth. "It's kinda high. I've never jumped off a waterfall before."

"It's only a baby waterfall." Cooper winks at me, his smile waking dormant places inside me.

I snicker and shake my head, dipping my chin so he can't see my blush.

"Do you remember those trees we used to scramble through? We found that lookout from the top of the pine up on Deer's Peak. Remember that?" Cooper takes another step toward me, his eyes gentle with affection. "The girl I used to know wasn't afraid of heights."

My nose wrinkles. "I think I just pretended so I didn't embarrass myself in front of you."

His eyebrows rise, and he tips his head like he's mulling over my words. I kind of love that he's slow to answer; it makes whatever he says more meaningful.

I watch him. My heart is chewed gum—soft and stretchy, yearning to reach out and stick itself to his, be one like we used to be.

"Well, you know, if you don't want to jump, you don't have to."

How sweet is that?

I wince. "But I kinda do."

"You don't have to give in to the pressure. This is your call."

Yeah, I'm definitely still in love with him.

"I miss being brave," I whisper, my eyes glassing over for a second. I blink and suck in a breath. "You probably don't want to hear this, but you made me brave when we were kids. You weren't afraid of anything."

He swallows, his look filled with so many things he's never going to say. I want to drown in that gaze, study it, memorize it, until I understand every little nuance.

With a quick blink, he breaks contact like he's suddenly aware of the window he just opened. His eyelids slam it shut, and he's back to the cool, calm expression that gives nothing away.

Holding out his hand, he gives me a smile, his voice husky when he asks, "Together?"

I want to jump into his arms and kiss him but suffice with placing my palm against his. As his fingers curl around my hand, I realize I've found home again. I forgot how much I love this familiar feeling.

He helps me up the rocks, and we appear together at the top.

"Finally!" Varam shouts, throwing his hands in the air.

"Yes! Jump, girl! Jump!" Leo laughs and claps.

Cooper grins at me, then walks for the edge. "Let's do this, Smoky."

With a high-pitched scream, I take the plunge, the air rushing past me and sucking the sound away. Cooper lets go of my hand, and we hit the water in sync. I close my mouth just in time, but water still shoots up my nose.

I surface, spluttering and flicking away wet locks that have stuck to my face.

People are cheering around me, and I'm looking for Cooper, but he's swimming for the edge of the water hole already. He gets out of the water, droplets running down his fine body as he grabs a towel and dries himself.

He is so freaking gorgeous.

I manage to catch his eye and score myself a very quick wink and smile that makes my insides trill. But then Teagan pops up beside him, squeezing water from her ponytail and dipping her hip in that flirty way of hers. Cooper smiles at her, but it's a polite expression, not the look he gave me before.

I should be comforted by that, but I'm kind of not.

I want to be the girl standing next to him. I want this group to know that he's mine and I'm his and that's the way it's always been.

"Well, that was nice of him." Varam appears, treading water beside me. "I could have held your hand for you, though. You just had to ask."

"Thanks." I give him a smile similar to the one Cooper's flashing Teagan, then make my way over to the safety of Leo and Shira.

Leo pulls me into a hug and whispers, "He was holding your hand! Was it electric?"

"Freaking fireworks!" I whisper with a grin, and we squeeze each other in that knowing, excited way only best friends can.

19

IT'S A NO-WIN

Cooper

IT'S PAST MIDNIGHT, and most of the island has settled.

I can still hear faint laughter from a bungalow near the restaurant. It's not Ashlyn's. Hopefully she's tucked up in bed and dreaming of sugar plum fairies or something.

Can't believe it's Christmas tomorrow.

Another one is coming and will be gone. Just another twenty-four-hour period with no special significance for me.

That'd probably make Grandpa Ray really sad. He always put in the biggest effort for Christmas. I guess he was making up for lost time—all those years where my mother rejected her parents. She let them back in for a while, when I was a baby, but then Dad got injured at work and he turned into a mean drunk, so she cut them off again to hide her shame.

Thankfully for us, in her dying days, she wrote her father a letter, explaining everything… and he came to rescue us not long after her funeral.

He was our personal savior, and we five, scared, lost boys happily ran away with him. Ran to the ranch where we got a glimpse of how freaking amazing life could be.

"Here." Jazz hands me a string of tinsel, and I climb the ladder, attaching it to the beam where she tells me to.

Judah and Bembe are working on the tree, but they keep getting told off by Jazz.

"Not there!" She bustles over to them, slapping Bembe's hands away and showing him exactly how to arrange the wrapped gift boxes.

I snicker, climbing back down the ladder and calculating how much more we have to do before we can get some shut-eye.

Christmas breakfast is always a special event on the island. The staff and guests eat together. The tables are set with red napkins and shiny cutlery. The best plates are brought out, and champagne flutes are filled for the Christmas toast.

It's a far cry from the cozy Christmases on the ranch. We'd stumble out of bed, following a jumping Brody and sleepy-eyed Deeks down the stairs, where Grandpa would be waiting by the tree.

"Look what Santa brought us!" He'd pat his belly and laugh. "Ho! Ho! Ho!"

I'm not sure any of us believed in Father Christmas anymore, but we kept pretending for the twins, just in case.

Brody would dive over the banister, landing with a thud and a roll before scrambling over the couch, then getting reprimanded for treating the furniture like a playground.

"Go back and do that again." Grandpa would point to the dining table, where Brody would walk back with a huff and stomp around the couch before plopping on the floor right by the tree.

Then we'd each get our turn unwrapping presents. The gifts were always thoughtful. Some of them handmade, others bought from town. Homemade cookies from Aunt Nell would always be in the mix, but then she'd show up sometime during the day with a sack full of toys as well.

"You spoil them." Grandpa would shake his head.

"Someone has to." She'd nudge him, and they'd laugh together.

Some years we'd go to Aunt Nell's and Uncle Thomas's for Christmas dinner; other years they'd come to us.

Christmas music from the 50s and 60s would play throughout the day. Brody and Jake would get hyped up on candy canes and wooden sword fights. Deeks would jump in because he couldn't help himself, and then an argument would no doubt ensue.

Every year.

Every. Single. Year.

That's kind of how the annual football in the snow

started. One big blowout that ended up dragging all five of us into it. Michael and I were trying to break things up but got caught in the tussle as well...

"That's it!" Grandpa bellowed above the ruckus. "Outside! All of you!"

"But it's..." Jake looked to me, double-checking he wasn't the only one who knew how cold it was. "It's... uh... It's snowing."

"So suit up. You get out there and work every other day of the year."

"You're putting us to work? That's bull—" Deeks swallowed the rest of his sentence before he had to start doing push-ups. His cheeks turned red with the effort not to explode.

I smirked and rubbed my mouth when Grandpa's eyes started to twinkle. "I didn't say you were working today. All I said was suit up!"

"Suit up for what?" Michael asked.

Grandpa grinned and grabbed a football. "It's time for a little Barrett boys fun!"

We scrambled, and ten minutes later we were out in the snow, hurling that ball through the air and playing the most unorganized game of football you've ever seen. The ball was up for grabs—whoever could get to it first picked it up and ran. Anyone could tackle anyone.

By the time we were done, our fingers were icy

sausages and our cheeks were red from smashing into the snow. But man, were we happy.

Hot chocolates next to the fireplace was the end of our day. Grandpa's deep voice soothed us to sleep as he read one of his favorite Christmas books and made us believe in miracles.

"Bembe!" Jazz laughs, the sound cutting my memories short and bringing me back to reality with a sharp slap.

No wintery fires in this place. We've tried to make the restaurant look magical with tinsel and fairy lights, but you can't have a cozy Christmas in this heat. It's just not the same.

I carry the ladder back to the storage room off the kitchen, unable to stop myself from thinking about Deeks, Michael, Jake, and Brody. I wonder how they spend their Christmases now?

Do Jake and Brody hang out with the foster family who took them after Grandpa died? Hopefully they still keep in touch. They seemed like nice people... well, the little glimpse I got of them anyway.

Deeks and Michael had the harder road with that group home, but hopefully they made some friends at community college or on their first jobs. Damn, I hope they went to some kind of college or got a good first job.

I hope they're okay. Safe. Happy. Content with life.

Please let them be. Let them all be good!

My hands are shaking as I wrestle the ladder back into

its home between the wall and the set of shelves. Squeezing them into fists, I cut the thoughts off and try to think of something else.

Anything else.

Ashlyn.

She flitters through my brain without me even trying, like she's permanently living there and just hides occasionally when I'm really distracted.

Shit.

It was so nice interacting with her today, I nearly forgot why I left in the first place.

Killer. You're no good for her.

I let the words settle in, sinking through my brain and right into my chest until I'm feeling them and acknowledging how real they are.

I shouldn't have flirted.

It was unfair.

I knew it the second she placed her hand in mine. The sparks that traveled through me were electrifying…and I couldn't let go. She was counting on me to get her over that waterfall. The second I knew she could handle it, I dropped her hand and swam away as soon as we'd hit the water. I was crossing a boundary that I'd specially erected for myself.

What the hell is wrong with me?

No good can come from my weakness. I have to be strong and keep her at arm's length. And the whole yo-yo thing I'm springing on her is just plain mean. It's best if I treat her like every other guest on this island. That's my job.

It doesn't matter that we still have feelings for each other.

She doesn't know the truth about what happened.

I'd mentioned my father a few times in the past, but I tried to make light of it, protect my brothers and Grandpa. The more I trusted Ashlyn, the more I let her in. She listened with horror and sympathy, even cried for me when I told her about Mom.

But what would she say if she knew what I'd done?

That adoring look in her eyes would die.

As it should.

I'm not the guy she used to know.

I wish there was an easy way of telling her that. A way that wouldn't hurt.

No matter what I do now, I can't win.

I never could.

I made my choice the night I pulled that trigger... and I will forever have to live with the consequences of my decision.

20

TIME TO MAKE A PHONE CALL

Ashlyn

CHRISTMAS EVE WAS A BUST. After the waterhole, we went back to the resort, and I didn't see Cooper again. He didn't work the bar that night, and I wouldn't have been shocked to find out he purposely hung out in the staff quarters just to avoid me.

The sudden switch-up was like whiplash, but again... I shouldn't be surprised.

Cooper made it clear from the second I saw him that he didn't want to let his guard down, but I picked at it anyway. I couldn't freaking help myself, and his defenses were weakened.

But then he just builds those walls back up again and I'm back to pining for a man I can't have.

I tried to distract myself at the Christmas Eve party. We danced, played silly drinking games, and laughed our asses off, but I couldn't get Cooper completely out of my brain, and I ended up dreaming about him.

We were standing at the top of a pine tree together, my hair blowing in the wind. He held my face and kissed me, his thumb caressing my jaw, his lips doing crazy things to my heart. But then he pulled away and looked at me with those sad eyes of his. Letting me go, he spread his arms wide and tipped backward, falling from the tree.

I screamed and reached out to grab him, but it was too late. He was gone.

I woke with tears in my heart and a quaking stomach.

Leo was snoring loudly, and I gazed at him in the darkness, wondering how I'd ever get back to sleep.

Why did Cooper leave?

What happened that night his Grandpa died? Or the nights following? He stayed around until the funeral and then just vanished. Aunt Nell could never tell me much, because she didn't know either...

"We just woke up and he was gone. He's taken his things with him, so we know he must have run away. I'm sorry I didn't tell you earlier, honey. I've been trying to look after the boys. They're devastated, and it's been hard enough getting them settled with new families and in a group

home. I can't believe they've been split up. It's so cruel."
Aunt Nell started to sniff and cry.

Selfishly, all I could murmur was "Cooper's gone?"

"I've told the sheriff about it, and he said he'd keep his
eyes open and an ear to the ground, but I can't shake the
feeling that Cooper doesn't want to be found. He hasn't
been the same since that night his grandpa died. I don't
know what happened at that ranch, but none of the boys
are coping, and it was obviously all too much for Cooper
to handle."

I couldn't bring myself to believe her, so I convinced
my parents to fly me to Montana, let me have a week off
school. But the visit did no good. I moped around for
days, crying over my lost love and the tragedy of losing
Ray Barrett. He was such a good man. Cooper adored him.
His heart must have been so broken. Was that why he
fled?

It's so weird that he left his brothers. He was a loyal
person, serious, believed in duty. He was so protective
over his siblings and he… he split.

His brothers deserve to know where he is.

But there's no cell phone reception on the island.

You know Aunt Nell's number. Find a phone and use it!

Surely the office will have some way of contacting the
outside world. Maybe if I say it's a family emergency or
something.

Whatever, I'll make it up when I get there.

I toss and turn for the next few hours, dozing in and out of sleep as the resolve settles into an immovable decision. As soon as I can, I'm calling to let the Barrett boys know I've found their brother.

I must drift back to sleep, because when I wake, light is brightening the walls and casting a soft glow over the bed.

Flinging back the covers, I rush to get ready. I don't bother being quiet. My haste is making me thoughtless. By the time I've finished with a subtle layer of makeup, Leo is sitting up in bed.

I walk out of the bathroom and spot his cheerful smile. "Merry Christmas, sweet thing."

"Merry Christmas." I grin, bending down to kiss him.

"Are we getting ready to gorge ourselves on Christmas breakfast?"

I rub my jittery stomach, not sure I'll be able to eat anything. Not until I've called my aunt. She can pass a message on for me, plus she's wise. Maybe she can help me figure out what to do.

"Well, wait for me." He jumps out of bed, tugging his palm tree pajama shirt straight. I don't know where he finds these clothes, but he's a master of color and pizazz. Even his pajamas make a statement.

"Actually, I'm just gonna make—"

"Girl." His pointing finger shuts me up. "I'll be fast."

He runs into the bathroom while I roll my eyes and figure delaying this call by a few minutes won't kill me. From the clatter in the bathroom, I can tell Leo really is rushing, so I do him the courtesy of sticking around until he breezes out, smelling fine and looking fresh.

"Very nice." I tweak the collar of his floral shirt, brushing my fingers down the green and red fabric.

"I've been saving it for today." His head wiggle and proud smile make me laugh.

"Come on, you." Threading my arm through his, I pull him out the door and we bump into Lance, Varam, Shira, and Mel.

"Hey, beautifuls!" Leo greets them all, handing out hugs and kisses like he's Santa's little elf.

"I am so looking forward to breakfast." Lance growls. "I'm freaking hangry."

"Can you smell it?" Shira breathes deeply. "Oh yeah, baby."

I join the group, placing myself between Mel and Leo so Varam can't brush his arm against mine while we're walking. As we near the stairs that lead down to the restaurant, I spot the sign to the main office and quickly divert course.

"Hey! Where are you going?" Shira stops me.

I turn, pointing over my shoulder with a sweet smile. "Just want to make a quick phone call."

They look at me like I'm crazy. We all went on and on about how the island was our getaway from the outside world, and here I am trying to get back into it after only a couple days.

"It's Christmas." I shrug. "I want to check in with my aunt."

"Wait a second." Leo whips off his shades to give me a

concerned frown. "Is this the one you visited over Thanksgiving? Girl, are you not telling us something? Is she dying and you just didn't want to say?"

"No." I bulge my eyes. "She's great. I mean, she's old, but she's fine. I just…" I shrug again, desperately trying to ooze casual. "She's my favorite aunt. She loves Christmas."

My excuse is lame. Favorite aunts can obviously wait until we get back to New York, but what else can I say?

Shira snorts. "I'm not planning on calling my parents. They'll be obsessing over their grandkids right now." She pulls a face like this is something gross. "They can just wish me Merry Christmas and Happy New Year on the same day."

Lance chuckles and kisses her head. "Love you, baby."

Varam gives me a hopeful grin, stepping away from the group and up toward me. "You want me to come with you? I might call my father after you're done."

"No, I'm good." I take a step away from him and smile to soften the move. "Please don't be offended. I just want to make this call in private."

Leo's ears perk up, his eyes narrowing for a second before he gives me an exaggerated wink.

Oh no. He's jumping to the wrong conclusions.

I know how his brain works. He now thinks I'm bluffing about the phone call and really I'm just making an excuse to get away and secretly meet up with Cooper.

I should correct him, but…

"Come on, V. You can save her a seat, honey." Leo tugs

on Varam's shirt, glancing over his shoulder and giving one more excited grin.

I cringe when he turns his back but take the chance to race to the reception area.

"Merry Christmas." The elegant lady behind the counter smiles at me. "How can I help you this morning?"

"Good morning." I brush my hands over the shiny countertop. "I need to call my aunt in Montana. It's kind of important."

"Absolutely." She starts arranging the phone so I can reach it, then goes into the details of how this is an extra expense and how much it will cost.

I nod and give her my bungalow number, not really caring about the price.

This is important.

"Thank you." I take the receiver and angle the phone away for privacy. I don't really need to, because just as I'm dialing, that French manager comes bustling in.

"Greta, what is this about a boat heading for the island? "

"It's probably just a day cruise, but I thought I should alert you anyway. You know how people love to island hop."

Maurice groans. "Let's just hope they redirect and keep cruising. The resort already feels full to overflowing, and Christmas is such a busy day."

"I'll keep you posted."

He nods and exits in a rush, not even noticing me as he calls over his shoulder, "I'm giving the Christmas toast in twenty minutes, so make sure you're there. I don't want to raise our glasses until everyone on the island is present."

Greta grins. "Yes, sir."

The door slides shut and Greta glances my way, then averts her gaze when I ping straight and say, "Aunt Nell?"

"Ashlyn? Is that you, honey? I thought you were somewhere in the Caribbean."

I laugh. Hearing her voice always fills me with so much joy. Nostalgia whistles through me, a deep pining I barely understand following closely in its wake. Why am I homesick for a place I've never actually called home?

I'm in paradise. Montana is miserable this time of year. Yet still.

"I miss you."

"Oh, bless you, sweet girl. Merry Christmas!"

"You too." I laugh. "And to Uncle Thomas."

"I'll pass it on. Now, tell me, where are you calling from?"

"I'm in the Caribbean… on this beautiful island. It's gorgeous."

"Sun. Sand. Heat. Is it everything you wanted?"

"And more."

She laughs. "Well, you be sure to take lots of pictures for me."

"I will. I…" My voice falters. Why do I feel like crying all of a sudden?

"You what, sweetie?"

I swallow, rubbing my forehead and blinking rapidly.

"Ashlyn. Are you okay?"

"Cooper's here," I whisper, ducking my head like I'm a spy relaying some kind of secret message.

"What?"

"Cooper. He's here."

Aunt Nell takes a minute to absorb what I just said. When she finally speaks, her voice is a breathy whisper. "Cooper Barrett?"

"Yes. He works on the island."

"You found Cooper? He's alive! Oh Lord, what an answer to my prayers! Praise Jesus, honey. You found him!"

"I did."

"You were meant to go to that island. This is providence right here!" Her voice rises with a joyous excitement that's almost contagious. "How's he doing?"

"He... well, he... He looks really good."

"I bet he does." She laughs. "But how's he really doing?"

I let out a defeated sigh. "To be honest, I don't know. It's like he wants to talk to me but doesn't. Like he's stopping himself from reconnecting."

"Have you told him about his brothers?"

"Not yet."

"Oh, Ashlyn, sweetie. You can't keep that to yourself. You have to tell him exactly what's going on at the ranch. He has a right to know."

"I don't know if he wants to know. That's the thing. He's pretty guarded."

"Sweet girl, if *anyone* can get through to that man, it's

you. You've always had a way with him. He let you in once. He's gonna do it again."

"How do you know that?"

"Because I haven't been praying this long for nothing. You're gonna bring the final Barrett boy home." She sounds so confident, like getting Cooper to fly back to Montana is the easiest thing in the world.

"I don't know if I can."

"*Yes*, you can. You don't believe anything else, you hear me? These boys need their big brother back."

I close my eyes, leaning my elbow on the counter and nodding. "I know they do."

Their faces swim through my mind, their joy at being back on the ranch mingled with the pain of what they lost. Their desperate hope to reunite the family was so strong when I saw them at Thanksgiving. They're on the cusp of that. I could help make it happen.

"Now, you tell me exactly which island you're on."

"Um… *Paradis Idyllique*. There's a website with contact details."

"Okay. I'll be sure to let the boys know. Now, you hang up this phone and go find yourself Cooper Barrett. You give us all a miracle this Christmas, sweet girl."

"I'll try."

"And you'll succeed. I just know it." Her confidence makes me smile. "I love you."

"I love you too."

She hangs up before I do, no doubt super keen to call the boys and give them the exciting news.

Crap, I hope I can make it exciting for them.

Nerves massacre my stomach as I hand the phone back with a shaky "Thank you" and head out the door. Rather than turning right, I make a left and sneak into the out-of-bounds area labeled Staff Only.

I'm breaking the rules, but it's for a very noble reason. Like I can hold this conversation in front of my friends. Cooper's going to need a private moment to process what I'm about to say.

Words slam through my brain, and I make two fists, struggling to come up with the perfect speech to pull him right back to a place he no doubt never wants to see again.

21

WHEN THE TRUTH IS TOO HARD TO HEAR

Cooper

I'VE BEEN UP since sunrise, trying to keep myself busy. Checking my watch, I calculate that I've got about fifteen minutes before I have to be in the restaurant for Maurice's Christmas toast. The guy likes to be on time and won't appreciate my lateness. It's a mission to coordinate an entire island of guests plus the staff. Thank goodness it only happens once a year.

My mental checklist is steadily being checked off as I try to avoid thoughts of Ashlyn and the fact that it's Christmas day. Will her friends have bought her presents? Will that tall douche lavish her with some expensive gift to win her over?

I frown and try to think about something else, but thoughts of boisterous boys tearing wrapping paper off gifts jump into my brain, and they're just as painful. The memory is only amplified when I turn the corner and am confronted by three squealing children conducting a water gun fight, the shiny plastic weapons telling me the gifts are getting immediate use.

"Don't shoot! Don't shoot!" I hold my hands up in surrender, putting on a big show and getting squirted anyway. Thankfully, the guns are pretty much empty, so my shirt only takes a small hit. "Merry Christmas, you little rug rats."

They run over to me, all talking at once as they try to show off their weapons and tell me about the other stuff Santa brought them.

"Not that Santa's real," Gisele whispers in my ear, obviously making sure I understand that she is much older and wiser than her brothers.

I wink at her, then crouch down next to Tajo so he can explain the intricacies of his water gun.

"Mine does that too," Maceo butts in, but he doesn't have a chance to say more because their mother comes bustling around the corner, speaking in a flurry of Spanish. I'm not exactly sure what she's saying, but by the looks on the kids' faces, they are getting seriously told off. Their heads droop before they jump to and race out of view.

I stand and give Amani a sympathetic smile. I get the impression parenting can be a really hard job, and Christmas morning is no exception.

"I told them they weren't allowed a water fight until *after* breakfast. Now we'll be late."

I chuckle and point to the corner they disappeared around. "They look to be hauling ass. You might still make it."

She starts to laugh. "I think I scared the daylights out of them. Better go check they haven't forgotten I'm mad." She wriggles her eyebrows and keeps laughing to herself as she walks away.

My grin fades as soon as she's out of sight. I wish I didn't have to go to breakfast. Ashlyn is going to be there, looking all beautiful, and I can't really talk to her. Well, I shouldn't anyway.

This sucks.

What I need is a decent hike away from this place. That's what I usually do to clear my head, but not on Christmas Day. I'm gonna have to suck it up. My reluctant body still hasn't moved, and I sway on my feet, trying to get my stubborn legs to budge.

The radio in my pocket blips. "Cooper, you there?"

Happy with the distraction, I grab it out and respond. "What's up, Maurice?"

"Looks like that boat is pulling in."

"You're kidding."

"I know. Of all the days, right? It's probably just a pleasure cruise docking for the morning, but I wanted to give you a heads-up. Have you had breakfast yet?"

"No, I was going to eat with everyone else."

"You've been up so long, I thought you might have grabbed something earlier." He sighs. "Okay, well, I'm toasting in ten minutes. Then you can quickly eat before getting back to work. Sorry about the rush, but I have no idea how many people are on this boat. We might need you on lifeguard duty around the pool or on the beach."

"No problem." I keep it light, actually kind of happy that I'll be so busy with extra guests, I won't even have the chance to talk with Ashlyn. My stomach clenches and I cringe. "I'll head to the restaurant now."

"Thank you. I'll get Rowena to go down and greet the boat, find out what they're planning, then let you know."

"Got it. Keep me posted."

"Will do."

I grip the radio in my hand and force my legs to move toward the restaurant. Better get this over with. At least I have every excuse to simply eat and run. I won't have a chance to—

"Ashlyn." I breathe her name more than say it, shocked to a stop by the sight of her.

She's looking stunning as per usual. The floaty, see-through dress covering her bikini is mouthwatering, so I look to the ground, scratching the back of my head and trying to stop my voice from shaking.

"This is, uh… this is actually a staff only area. Are you…?" I glance up, my thoughts derailing as I look at her face." Did you…? Did you, um…?"

She licks her lips, giving them a glossy shine that I can't take my eyes off. "I know I'm supposed to be at breakfast. I just…" Her teeth scrape her bottom lip. I spot the tremble of her chin and am instantly alert.

Moving to her without thinking, I gently touch her elbow. "Are you okay?"

She nods, but the sheen in her vibrant eyes tells me she's lying.

"What is it?"

With a thick swallow, she grabs my hand. I fumble the radio I'm holding and catch it against my leg. My hand is shaking as I place it down on the railing and turn to face her. She takes my other hand, rubbing her long thumb over my knuckles. We're facing each other like we're standing at an altar about to exchange wedding vows. The look on her face is deep with meaning and emotion.

I don't know what the hell she's about to say to me, but I can barely breathe. The electricity flowing between us is super charged. How is my hair not standing on end right now?

"I know you don't really want to talk to me, but there are things I have to tell you."

That statement hurts. Of course I want to talk to her!

I just can't.

I wish I could make her understand, but then I'd have to tell the truth, and I can't bear the thought of her knowing.

"I… I…" Struggling for air, I force the words out of me. "I wish I could talk to you. It's not that I don't want to, I just…" The rest of her statement finally catches up to me. "Wait. What do you mean? What things do you have to tell me?"

Her delicate eyebrows wrinkle. "It's about your family. Your brothers."

I snatch my hands back, taking a step away like she's just slapped me in the face. "How do you…?" I shake my head. "Have you seen…?"

I bite my lips together, desperate to ask yet not wanting to know.

What about my brothers? I want to take her shoulders and shake her with this urgent plea, but I don't have a right to know!

Blinking rapidly, I spin away from her, running a hand through my hair and fisting the back. My eyes feel like needles are being poked into them. I'm not sure I can handle this. I'm minutes away from a room full of guests and staff. And there's a new boatload of people to deal with. I can't do this right now!

"Please, Cooper, you—"

"It's a really busy morning for me," I cut her off, spinning with an apologetic smile. "All hands on deck kind of thing. That's what… Maurice needs me to, uh… Can we talk about this later?" I nod, feeling like an asshole as I point past her and try to get out of this. "Merry Christmas, Ashlyn."

Brushing past her hurts, but I'm three full steps away before she stops me with a statement I never thought I'd hear.

"They're looking for you."

I jerk, my eyes bulging as my heart thunders out of control.

"They've all come back home, to the ranch, and they want you there with them."

What?

I spin to face her, unable to hide my surprise, my repulsion at that idea. "No." I shake my head. "They wouldn't go back there. They... they wouldn't do something that stupid. It's... They—"

"They have." She nods. "They've made it their home again, and they want you with them. Cooper, it's time for you to go back to Montana."

I'm shaking my head before she's even finished talking. "I... I can't. I—"

I'm not sure what to say. How do I explain myself?

I feel like a row of charges is being set off in my brain, one explosion after the other, but then...

A rapid spray of gunfire fills the air, followed by a wave of terrified screaming.

Wait. That's not in my head.

That's real.

I flinch and duck, my instincts reaching for Ashlyn and yanking her to the ground with me.

"What was that?" she squeaks, her eyes bulging as more gunfire echoes from the direction of the beach followed by a second flurry of screams.

22

TERROR

THAT WAS GUNFIRE.

Holy shit!

People are screaming. I can hear their terror floating back to the staff quarters.

What the hell is going on?

Cooper's hand is on my back. He's keeping me down, his body taut as he crouches beside me, looking around and assessing the situation.

I glimpse his face, the intense expression, the way he's robotically taking it in before flying into action. Cooper was always able to do that. Emergencies brought out a calm efficiency in him that made me kind of jealous.

My hands are trembling. My entire body is a shaking mess, my nose tingling with tears as my heart plays heavy bass between my ears.

What is happening?

Are we gonna die?

Panic claws at me.

"Cooper," I whisper, but he cuts me off with a finger to his lips.

More gunfire makes me squeeze my eyes shut. Distant shouting and screams burn through me, the shakes I'm fighting amplified when the sound of running feet draws near.

"Let's move," Cooper whispers so softly I barely hear him. Snatching my arm, he hauls me up and rushes us around the side of a building.

"Check every room! No strays! Gather them in the restaurant!" someone shouts.

Cooper shoves me into a narrow gap between two buildings, slipping in behind me and pressing his finger to his lips again.

I nod, biting my chattering teeth together and trying not to breathe.

Shit. Shit. Shit!

Cooper's fingers curl around my waist, squeezing lightly when the sound of running feet shoots right past us.

I don't know how long we wait it out in that spot, but it feels like an eternity. My head is pounding, and each fresh spurt of gunfire, shouted word, and cry of fear makes my stomach clench.

Tears are trailing down my cheeks, and I'm too afraid to move or brush them away.

Please don't find us. Don't find us!

I rest my head against the rough concrete and wait it out. I'm not sure how long we'll have to stay here, but my thoughts are with my friends.

They're in the restaurant, no doubt cowering from these men with guns.

Have any of them been shot?

Are any of them dead?

I have to help them!

A fresh wave of terror engulfs me, my chin trembling as my eyes burn and set another stream of tears free.

Why is this happening?

What do these people even want?

And how the hell are we going to get out of this?

23

STUBBORN DETERMINATION MIGHT GET YOU KILLED

Cooper

I DON'T KNOW what the hell is going on right now. All I can hear is my heart pounding in my eardrums as I try to think straight and figure out what to do.

I'm still reeling from what Ashlyn just told me. My brothers are back at the ranch. How? How could they go back to that place? They want me there with them. I don't understand.

And I don't have time to process any of it, because there's gunfire, screaming, Ashlyn's terrified breath whistling against my ear. Her breathing is too fast. Too loud.

As gently as I can, I press my finger against her lips.

They're trembling. Her green eyes dart to mine and I hold her gaze, trying to anchor us both with a calm I'm far from feeling. We're sandwiched in a narrow gap between two buildings, her back pressed against the wall while I rest my hand by her shoulder, blocking her from sight as best I can. She's so close. So scared. So damn beautiful.

I swallow, then wince, paranoid about making any sound that might give us away. Footsteps are still racing around nearby. This hiding spot is good, but if they find us, we've got nowhere to run. I need to get Ashlyn out of here.

Faint screams reach me again, and my stomach clenches. *Don't let anyone be dead.* I think of the three kids, Amani, Juan, my friends on staff, Maurice, Rowena, all the people I work with. Not to mention the guests on the island. Are they being held hostage or are they just dead?

Is this an act of terror or ransom?

I need to find out.

I need to get Ashlyn to safety then call for help.

Counting to one hundred, I hold my breath, then slowly peek my head into the open. All seems quiet and clear. Maybe this is a good place to hide.

But I can't call for help.

I need to get to the one place I know houses a telephone—the admin block.

"Where are you going?" Ashlyn snatches my wrist, her urgent whisper punchy.

Keeping my movements smooth and easy, I turn back to face her. "I have to call for help. I need to get to a phone and alert the authorities at Saint Martin."

"Okay," she squeaks, her expression the epitome of fear.

"You stay here and—"

"No. You can't leave me here alone. You can't leave me. I'm coming with you."

"It'll be safer if you—"

"I'm coming with you." The determined glint in her eye tells me this is a lost argument, but I try anyway.

"I don't want you to get hurt."

"I'm coming with you." She whispers it again, and I know from past experience that she'll keep doing that until she gets her way.

I never could say no to her, and if I ever tried, this is what I got—stubborn determination.

A soft snicker punches out of me, but it's swallowed away by dread, thick and sinister. Squeezing my eyes shut, I huff and shake my head.

"Mule," I mutter under my breath.

"Ass," she counters, whipping me back into the past for a brief second.

The memory is a sweet comfort, and I reach for her hand, pulling in a calming breath before leading us out into the open.

We take it slow, ducking and weaving our way to the reception area. There are a couple routes and I take the long one, which is more obscure and only used by a few of the staff.

By the time I'm pressing my back against the wall of the admin block, sweat is peppering my forehead and soaking into my shirt. I'm not overly hot, but terror obviously makes my pores leak or something. Ashlyn's hand is slick in mine. I squeeze her long fingers, giving her a reassuring nod as we ease our way around the building.

We haven't been spotted, and I haven't seen anyone either. I don't know how to feel about that. Warning bells are faintly ringing in the back of my mind, and I pull up short when I hear someone shouting from Maurice's office.

"I want that phone ready to go in ten minutes!"

I frown and lean my head around the corner to glance through the glass window.

"Got it, boss." A thin guy in a checkered shirt is opening a laptop and plugging stuff in. I don't know anything about tech, but I'm guessing he's trying to do something with the internet, maybe access the resort database or something.

"Get me a list too." A man storms out of Maurice's office, and I duck out of sight. He's a tall, imposing asshole with a dark beard and shaggy black curls. That one glimpse of him stirs ugly feelings in my chest. He reminds me of my father both in essence and looks, although I doubt my old man would be smart enough to pull off something like this. He did find us on the ranch, I guess, which is a mystery I'll never figure out. We were there for eight years, safely hidden away. My mother never told him where she came from, which meant he had zero clues to go on, so how'd his drunken ass find out?

"I know there's a bunch of rich pricks on this island right now, and I want to know everything about them!

Check everyone off and make sure they are all in the restaurant."

"Hey, boss."

A radio blips and he snatches it off the counter, snarling into the speaker, "What?"

"We've got some hysterical guests down here. This Asian dude won't stop wailing, and this chick keeps screaming at us that we have no right to be here."

"Shut them up and keep them under control. I don't care what you have to do."

"But you told us not to shoot them dead."

"There are other ways to silence them! A bullet wound to the arm, a broken kneecap, or a punch to the face isn't going to kill anyone. Scare them shitless and shut them up!"

Ashlyn lets out a choked gasp, her fingers fisting my shirt as she presses her mouth into my shoulder and whimpers. I brush my hand down her arm and nudge her in the direction we came from. There's no way I can get access to the phone, so it's back to hiding and figuring out a new plan.

Leading her back through the rabbit warren of pathways, I make it safely to the staff quarters. We duck behind a building to scope the area. Things are quiet, and we risk a quick run to my studio apartment.

I never bother locking my door, so I shove it open and power through.

"Who are—"

"Shh." I quiet her, trying to close the door without

making a sound, then quickly scan the room and look out each window.

My bed's not made.

Crap. This place is a mess.

I shouldn't care, but Ashlyn's standing right there, looking at the unwashed dishes in the sink, the books stacked haphazardly around my bed, and the pile of yet-to-be-washed clothes spewing out of the basket.

I'm not normally like this, but work got busy and I've hardly been in my room lately, and—

With a huff, I snatch the clothes up and shove them properly in the basket, then start rearranging the books into neat piles, like it matters. Like this is important right now.

"Who are those guys?" Ashlyn whispers.

I stand up and straighten my shirt, running a hand through my hair as I pace around the bed and pull the covers straight. "No idea. But I'd like to know why they want a guest list."

"He said 'rich pricks.' It must be a money thing." Ashlyn blinks rapidly, running her hands up and down her arms like she's cold.

I search for a hoodie, but I'm not even sure where one is. It never gets cold enough on the island for a sweater.

"Your friends *are* super rich," I mutter, hunting in my closet and coming up empty-handed.

Ashlyn snorts. "Well, their *parents* are."

I turn to give her a decisive nod. "Ransom."

"Yeah." Her voice trembles, but she tries for a hopeful smile. "So they're not going to kill anybody."

I nod again. "As long as they get what they want."

Her smile wavers and drops away.

Shit, I shouldn't have said that.

She bites her bottom lip, her chin trembling a little as she bobs her head. "We need to help them."

"As soon as a ransom call goes out, help will be on its way. I need to get you out of here. We have to get off this island." Snatching my running shoes, I kick off my flip-flops and gear up for a sprint across the island. There's a fishing boat moored in a private cove about two miles from the resort. We can take an isolated back trail that not many know about. As long as we can get away from the resort, undetected, we can—

"Get me out of here? What?" Ashlyn's confused frown makes my own form.

What does she not understand?

I give her a little more detail. Maybe that's what she's wanting. "We can sneak out the back gate. I'll—"

"I'm not leaving my friends." Her emphatic voice warns me that an argument is brewing.

Dammit!

"Are you crazy? We're not going back for your friends. There are armed gunmen everywhere."

"Who are going to hurt them if we don't do something to stop this."

"And what do you expect us to do?" I shoot her an incredulous look.

She opens her mouth to argue back, but nothing comes out. Her eyes dart the room like she has no idea.

I shake my head and go back to putting my shoes on. I

tie the laces of my sneakers nice and tight, focusing on the double knot before looking back up at her.

She's clenching her jaw, eyeing me with a look I've seen before.

No! I can't let her win this. I don't care how stubborn she is. She's not thinking this through.

Crossing her arms, she gives me that glint of determination, but I shake my head against it.

"I don't care what you think. I'm not leaving my friends. I am not leaving them."

No! She can't freaking "repeat phrase" her way out of this.

We don't have time for this shit!

"Ashlyn." My voice is firm, like a reprimanding parent, but I don't frickin' care. I'm not letting her risk her life. There are safer ways to go about this, and getting off the island is top priority.

Standing tall, I approach her with quick steps, ready to throw her over my shoulder if I have to.

She backs away and points at me. "I am *not*—"

The door crashes open. The first thing I see is a handgun, followed by a guy with broad shoulders and a neck tattoo. Ashlyn's sentence dissolves into a scream, and I move without thinking.

Charging the guy, I wrap my hand around the slide of his gun, slapping his wrist with my other hand. He's disarmed before he can blink, the gun now securely in my grasp. Using it like a baton, I crack the side of his head with the butt and catch his shoulder as he crumples.

He hits the floor with minimal impact, and I lay the

gun behind him so I can start searching his body when the sound of running feet alerts me to the fact that more men are on their way. I stand, grab Ashlyn's wrist, and run for the window. Sliding it open with a grunt, I push her through and support her arm so she doesn't land with a crash on the concrete path outside.

"Hey!" someone shouts at my disappearing back as I leap out the window and snatch Ashlyn's hand.

Breaking into a sprint, I pull her toward the back gate.

I don't care what she wants to do.

I'm getting her off this island.

I have to.

Because the thought of someone hurting her freaking kills me.

24

SWEET MEMORIES AND SCALDING TRUTHS

Ashlyn

COOPER'S PULLING SO HARD I feel like my arm will rip out of its socket. But I don't tell him to stop, because there are men with guns behind us. They're shouting and angry, and Cooper disarmed that guy like he was a freaking action hero. When the hell did he learn to do that?

My sandals slip as we jump off the path and along the dirt track, leading to some kind of side gate that only staff must know about. The gold straps dig into my flesh, biting and hurting, but I don't have time to stop and take them off.

A bullet pings off the palm tree next to me. I scream

and duck my head. Cooper pulls a little harder and I cry out, unable to hide my pain.

"Are you hit?" He whips around, fear stark on his face.

I shake my head. I can't speak. I'm being chased by a man with a gun. A bullet just missed my head. My friends are being held hostage by these psychopaths.

Holy shit! Holy shit!

Cooper urges me forward, his silent, sure way settling my nerves a little. Okay, a very little. I am freaking out!

We reach the gate, Cooper slamming his shoulder into it as soon as the bolt is pulled free. Rushing down the narrow trail, we plunge into the jungle, and all I can hope is that he knows where he's going, that we can find a good place to hide until these guys give up and we can safely sneak back into the resort so I can free my friends.

Because I'm not leaving them.

I don't care what kind of argument Cooper's gonna make. I can't just look out for number one. They're my friends. I won't cut and run! How can I possibly abandon them when they might be getting their kneecaps smashed in?

Another spray of bullets scatters the ground at my feet.

I pick up my pace, ignoring the pain between my toes as these stupid sandals argue with this physical activity.

What the hell are you doing running? You never run, let alone sprint like some maniac! Calm the hell down and walk like you normally do!

I push on, adrenaline and instinct driving me forward.

I can't die.

No one will be able to help my friends if I bleed out on some hidden pathway on the back of this island.

Cooper let my hand go as soon as we left the resort, and as much as I miss holding it, it's way easier to run. I pump my arms and try to keep pace with him, slapping big palm leaves and bright green foliage out of my way when he veers off the path.

We're running in dense jungle now—untamed island wilderness. It's a little off-putting, although Cooper seems to know what he's doing. I've always kind of loved that about him, trusted him blindly. Should I still be doing that?

Should I—

A surprised yelp punches out of me as Cooper grabs my wrist and flings us both off the edge of a small cliff.

It's not really a cliff. It's a boulder thing, and we plunge into water together. Kicking hard, I stay with him as he pulls me toward a cave. It's hard to swim with him holding me, so I wriggle out of his grasp and cut my arms through the water. Grabbing the back of my dress, he hauls me with him until we enter a cave opening.

Finding a hold on the edge, he grips it, then pulls me against him, wrapping his arm around my waist and drawing us into the shadows.

"Shhhh," he breathes in my ear, the deep tenor of his voice vibrating through me.

I cling to his shoulders, not missing the strength beneath my hands. He's always been strong. Even when we were young teens and his body was still developing, he had strength in him—taut muscles and a tenacity that wouldn't let him be anything but capable.

And now he's a man. Strong, calm, protective. A freaking warrior.

I tuck my head into the crook of his neck, my breath hitting his wet skin and rebounding back on me. Water droplets fall from his nose and land on my cheek. I close my eyes, focusing on the simple act of kicking my legs under water, trying to keep us afloat as much as possible.

Cooper is clinging to the rock and me, holding me steady, his strong arm locking me to his side.

If only the circumstances were different. Heat rushes through me, memories of our last summer together hitting me at the most inappropriate moment. That day we spent at the waterhole, hidden away like we were the only two people on the planet.

I've never been with anyone but him.

If I let my mind wander far enough, I can still feel his lips on my skin, the sensation of being completely, one hundred percent connected with another human being— body, mind, and soul. We let ourselves be vulnerable, our explorations tentative and sweet. It was an epic first time, and we spent the rest of the summer coming back for more. Cooper Barrett was my opium.

We were high on love. We were one.

And I've never gotten over it.

"Where'd they go?" A harsh voice jolts me back to reality.

"I heard a splash! They're in the water somewhere."

Gunfire peppers the pool we dove into. I flinch and

muffle my screams, pressing my lips against Cooper's neck and squeezing myself against him. He holds me tight, his muscles flexing, his sure body stopping me from losing my mind.

His steady legs kick beneath the water as we hold our breaths and press ourselves into the shadows.

It feels like an eternity as the men wait it out to see if any bodies float to the surface of the water.

"Shit!" one of them eventually spits. "You head that way. Check down the trail. Maybe they threw a rock in the water or something, trying to divert us."

"Or they swam across the other side."

"I'll go 'round and look."

"Don't forget to call it in."

A string of mumbled curses is followed by the click of a radio. "We've got a couple runners. They escaped out back, and we lost their trail. Over."

The voice on the other end is a little muffled, but I can still make out his shouting. "Find them! No one gets off this island unless I say so!"

Cooper clenches his jaw; I can feel the bone moving against my head. I don't dare shift to look at him. Instead, I grip his wet T-shirt that much tighter and pray those guys will hurry up and move.

Boots stomp away, and we wait another five minutes before finally swimming to the edge of the cave entrance. The second Cooper lets me go, I feel unexpectedly bereft, like I don't have the strength to do anything unless he's touching me.

It's a weird sensation and I berate myself for it, but it still doesn't leave me.

Kicking a little harder, I follow him out of the cave and take his hand when he helps me out of the water. Ditching my sandals, I fling them into the brush and brave nature with my bare feet. I have sissy winter feet right now, but it's got to be better than cutting straps and painful toes.

Creeping after Cooper, we quietly reenter the brush, heading back the way we came.

At least I thought we were, until we reach a wider trail that doesn't look a thing like the one we came down earlier.

"This way." Cooper tips his head and I follow him, scanning the area and trying to find my bearings.

"Where's the resort?" I glance behind me, doing a spin and taking in the thick foliage.

"We're not going to the resort. I'm taking you to a cove nearby. There's a fishing boat we can use to—"

"No!" I jerk to a stop, crossing my arms and no doubt looking petulant, but I thought I made myself very clear back in his apartment. "I am *not* leaving my friends."

Cooper stops, dipping his head and squeezing the back of his neck. The huffing sigh that comes out of him tells me what I need to know, but then he turns around and I get the full brunt of his emotion. "Ashlyn, we're not doing this. I won't let you talk me into being insane. We can't go back. We have to leave. I'm getting you somewhere safe."

I start shaking my head, but all that does is increase his volume.

"Yes we are! What do you want to do? Bust in there and take on a boatload of gunmen?"

"You managed to disarm that guy before. You made it look like a walk in the park."

He scoffs, looks to the sky, then makes two fists in the air like he's asking the god of patience for help and begging the god of common sense to enlighten me.

My nostrils flare and I change my stance, hoping I look strong and ready for battle.

He doesn't even notice. His eyes bore into me, a look of desperation wrinkling his forehead. "Bullets kill, Ashlyn. They will shoot you dead!" His voice breaks. "Now, you are not staying here."

"I'm not leaving."

He growls and storms toward me, snatching my wrist and trying to pull me after him. I wrench myself free.

"Don't do this." His husky voice is low with warning, but I meet his stare head-on.

"You can't stop me." I spin and head away from him, hoping this path leads back to the resort. But before I've made three steps, his arm is around my waist and he's lifting me off the ground.

"I'll carry you there if I have to."

"Put me down!" I screech, slapping at his arm. Damn his strength right now! Kicking my legs, I try to wriggle free, but he marches forward like I'm no more than a toddler throwing a tantrum. "I mean it, Cooper! Let me go!"

"Not until you're safe."

I let out an indignant scream, and then words start

spewing out of me. It's a hot, uncontrolled rant that doesn't hide one speck of truth. "I'm not you! I won't just cut and run when things get too difficult or scary. I'm not abandoning the people who need me right now!"

He goes still, his hold around my waist slackening until my feet land with a thud on the packed dirt.

His swallow is thick, and I'm almost scared to turn and face him.

Shit, what did I just say?

But I'm right! I won't abandon my friends. I won't just run away, because—

I turn to tell him that, but the look on his face about breaks my heart. It's only his profile, but the way he licks his trembling lips... the way he's running his fingers through his hair like that...

He can't even look at me, and I've momentarily lost all my fire... until he shakes his head and starts walking away!

25

CATASTROPHIC GUILT

Cooper

"OH REALLY?" she spits out behind me. "So that's it, you're gonna do it again? Just walk away? Because that always works out so well for everybody!"

I spin in time to see her long arm flicking into the air.

Her face, so stunningly beautiful, is puckered with anger, her long, wet hair sticking to her dress, which is completely see-through thanks to our dunk in the water. The fabric clings to her bikini, her waist, the perfect curve of her hips.

And I can't appreciate any of it.

Because she's mad at me. And maybe she has a right to be, but dammit, she doesn't know!

It's so obvious we're talking about my family right now, and it's hardly the time to have it out. Those men could be anywhere, circling back to the place they started and trying out a new direction. Yelling at each other could be alerting them to our location, so I keep my voice low and step toward her. "I did what was best for them."

"Bullshit!" She accentuates the T so the word feels like a stingy slap to the face. "They needed you. *I* needed you! And you just took off! You didn't even say goodbye."

"Shhh," I try to caution her, but I can tell by her heaving chest and fiery expression that nothing's going to calm her down in a hurry. I sigh and mutter, "You guys were better off without me."

"No we weren't! You broke my heart." She points at her chest, her words crumbling apart as she fights sudden tears. With a sharp sniff, she tries to rein in her emotions. "And as for your brothers… they got split up. Jake and Brody have been shifted around. Do you have any idea how many foster homes they had to put up with? And Michael, he…" She lets out a choked breath, then points at me. "Deeks nearly died! They both nearly died!"

A cold chill sweeps through me. Guilt is heavy, catastrophic.

I want to grab her shoulders and demand answers.

What happened?

How?

When?

Give me details!

I need to know everything.

But then I don't.

Covering my ears, I drop to my knees like a coward. My shame is so thick and suffocating, I'm buried under it, within it, gasping for air.

Deeks nearly died?

Michael... nearly died?

The twins. Foster homes.

But they were fine! They looked happy enough! I saw them laughing!

I'm blinded by images that my imagination is morphing into nightmares.

I didn't think—

I mean, I thought—

Ashlyn's feet come into view. I stare at her pretty toes with the shiny blue polish and the silver ring on her right foot.

She flicks my hands off my ears and speaks softly. "I know you don't understand and you think I'm totally illogical. But I can't turn my back on Leo and Shira... any of those people. Not when I could help. And I don't know how I can help, but I have to try."

My head moves in slow motion, glancing up to look at her.

She slashes tears off her cheeks and lifts her chin. "Are you coming?"

I can't move.

I can barely breathe.

My brothers nearly died. They suffered. I wasn't there to help them.

"Fine," Ashlyn clips.

Spinning on her heel, she takes off while I sway on my

knees and try to counter the grenade that just exploded in my belly.

What happened to my brothers? When I came back to check on them, they were okay. It was about two months after I'd left. The guilt was hounding me, so against my better judgment, I returned. I don't know what I was looking for—reassurance maybe. I hunted them down and played covert spy for nearly a week.

Jake and Brody were happy. They had a nice foster family looking after them. They were settled. Deeks and Michael were in the group home and attending high school. I thought they were okay. No blood or bruises to speak of, no yelling coming from the house they were staying in. They were walking to high school each day with bags and books. They looked like normal teenagers.

I mean, sure, all of them were obviously still mourning Grandpa, but they were healthy. They seemed all right.

If I'd walked back into their lives, I would have disrupted everything. I was eighteen. I had nothing. What kind of life could I have offered them? How could I seriously have asked them to be raised by a... a...

"A killer," I whisper, my mind catapulting back to that harrowing day I returned to the ranch...

It'd been over two months since that rainy night Grandpa died.

The ranch, our place of peace and comfort, had momentarily become a house of horrors.

I felt so sick walking up that long driveway, I nearly passed out when I reached the house. Gazing up at the empty structure, void of life and movement, turned my insides to stone. Still, I trembled as I tried to find a way in.

It took me a few minutes to remember the key under the stairs. I'd made a box in Grandpa's workshop, and he made a big deal out of my accomplishment. He always knew how to make us feel special, worthy.

My fingers trembled when I pulled the key free and unlocked the back door. He wouldn't have thought me worthy anymore. I probably had no right stepping foot in that house again. Not after what I'd done.

I walked through the empty kitchen, my boots echoing off the wooden floor. I was an iron robot, moving through the house with measured steps until I reached the living room. Leaning my thighs against the sheet-covered couch, I stared at the fireplace and that awful brown stain on the stones.

Blood.

Grandpa's blood.

I didn't hear my old man arrive that night. Shouting was the first thing to alert me to trouble, and initially I thought it was my brothers arguing over something stupid. But it was too chaotic. The tone had a sinister vibe that was foreign at the ranch, and then I heard Grandpa yelling, and that was so unusual. It wasn't his cheerful "Get to work" type yell. It was something different.

Fear tore through me so hot and fast, I raced for the gun cabinet. I wasn't planning on shooting anyone, but I wanted Grandpa to have access to the gun in case he needed it. He'd shown me where the key was. He'd trained me how to use the weapon for hunting. I knew how to clean, maintain, aim, and fire that gun. I was actually a damn good shot.

So, when I walked into the lounge and saw what was going down, I...

Grandpa was on the ground, his arms splayed wide, Michael and Jake crowding over him like he was dead or something. My father had Deeks in a headlock, and it looked like he was choking him to death.

I lifted that gun to my shoulder and took aim.

I didn't yell "Freeze!"—I didn't want that bastard to have the option of letting go.

I didn't go for a leg wound so the police could deal with him later.

No. In that moment, I wanted him *dead*. So I took a head shot—clean, simple, and decisive.

There was no way in hell he was getting up again after that.

And he didn't.

I killed him.

I killed my own flesh and blood.

It wasn't until after I'd squeezed the trigger and saw his body jerk and then flop to the floor that it really hit me. He landed with a dull thud, and it struck me like a punch to the face.

I'd just shot a man, not by accident but on purpose.

I'd intentionally taken someone's life.

What kind of person did that make me?

I stood there like a mute idiot, fear pulsing through me while I swayed on my feet. I wanted to fall apart but couldn't because my brothers were in a panic. Brody was saying something about covering it up, and I just went along with it, because I couldn't think straight.

Jake and Michael rushed Grandpa to the hospital, and as the rest of us buried my father's body up on the ridge and watched his truck careen down the embankment into the lake, I figured I could confess all to Grandpa when he woke up, and he'd tell me what to do.

But he never woke up.

The days following that night were a blur. I kept it all in for the sake of my brothers, but after Grandpa was laid to rest, standing at the funeral and hearing all those wonderful things said about the man I adored made me feel like a worthless piece of shit. I didn't deserve to be standing alongside my brothers. My grandpa would have been so ashamed of my choices. I couldn't face it.

Aunt Nell and Thomas were looking after the boys, so I slipped away into the night, knowing everyone would be better off without me.

And I was right. When I came back to check on them, they were. And when I went to visit the ranch, I knew we couldn't live there again. The pain within those walls would have killed us all.

I made the right choice.

I disappeared to give them all a real chance.

At least that's what I thought I was doing.

26

IMMOBILIZING TERROR

Ashlyn

I SLASH MORE tears off my face, frustrated by the fact that I'm crying at all. Like I have time for that right now. I need to find the damn resort and help my friends. I'm not sure how I'm going to do that with no radio, no weapon, and basically no idea what I'm doing. But I can't just sneak away when they could be getting beaten to a pulp.

I need Cooper.

Dammit!

I can't believe he just sat there!

The guy I used to know would have been the first to volunteer to save the day. He was a hero. He was... perfect.

"Nobody's perfect," I mutter, closing my eyes and feeling like an idiot for turning my memory of summer romance into something so much more.

Cooper had his faults. I had mine too.

I can't really remember what any of his were, except for the big fat one that I just threw in his face.

He left! He ran because he was scared or sad or... I don't know! He abandoned his people, and I'm not willing to do the same.

I blink at more tears and slow to a stop when I get to a fork in the trail.

Great! Which one leads back to the resort?

Shit, what am I doing?

I can't do this without Cooper!

But he doesn't want to help you, so you're just going to have to try!

Why did he leave his family?

What was the real reason behind his bizarre behavior? The Cooper I knew didn't walk away from a fight. He didn't crumple to his knees when challenged on his behavior.

Maybe the Cooper you knew doesn't exist anymore. Maybe he died the same night his grandpa did.

The thought makes my eyes burn all over again.

I sniff and impulsively take a left. That feels right, like it might be leading back to the resort.

Swiping my finger under my nose, I sniff and try to pick up my pace, but my poor bare feet are not happy with me. It's hard to walk quickly when rocks and roots keep digging in and catching me off guard.

Hissing at yet another stone in my foot, I flick it out and watch my step. In fact, I'm so intent on watching my step that I don't even notice the man in front of me until his boots come into view.

I jerk with a gasp, my eyes rounding as they travel up his body, over the gun in his beefy hands, and come to rest on his face. His pale eyes glint, and he tips his head with a leering smirk before reaching for me.

"No!" I scream and spin to run, but he snatches the back of my dress, the material making a sharp ripping sound when he pulls me off my feet.

I land on my butt with a hard thud, and after a second to absorb the pain, I scramble to my feet.

I don't even make it to a full stand before he's gripping my shoulder and trying to put me on the ground again.

"No!" I scratch and claw, making his job as difficult as possible.

Spinning me around, he slams my back into his chest, securing his arm around my shoulder to hold me still. He lets out a creepy laugh, his hand traveling south as he tries to check out the shape of my body.

Oh gross. No, no, no!

"Let me go," I squeak as I strain against him.

He's freaking strong, but I'm desperate, and when my attempt to smash my heel into his shin doesn't work, I put up with a little breast squeezing in order to wriggle around and bury my teeth into his upper arm.

"Argh!" His howl is pitched high with pain and he lets me go, but not for long enough.

When I try for a second escape, he grabs a fistful of my

hair, yanking hard and nudging my knee so I'm brought to the ground with another thud.

My arms scrape across the dirt, the air knocked out of me when he digs his knee into my back, then roughly spins me over. His fist hits me before I even see it coming. Blinding pain flashes across my face followed by a sharp ache in my cheek.

Holy crap!

I've never been punched before, and it freaking hurts.

Squeezing my throat, he straddles me and goes to hit me again, but I fling my arm up, slowing the blow. He clips the top of my head, his knuckles glancing off my scalp. The pressure on my throat increases, fear terrorizing me as I struggle for air.

No! No! I can't die right now! No!

Panic forces my instincts into overdrive. Scraping the ground around me, I hunt for any kind of weapon. When my fingers brush something solid, I grab at it and slash my arm toward him. The rock I'm holding smashes into the guy's head, loosening his hold on me.

Slightly dazed, he tips sideways and I wriggle free, kicking him between the legs as I crawl to my feet.

He groans, grabbing his crotch and crumpling to the ground. I scramble away, sprinting down the path before he can lay another finger on me.

"Get back here, you little bitch!"

I glance over my shoulder but don't slow down. He's rubbing blood off the side of his hair, then lets out an angry growl when he looks at his red fingers. I gasp when he stands up and starts hobbling after me.

"You're dead!"

Turning back, I pick up my pace and sprint as fast as I can. I'm not a runner. Hell, I'm probably one of the most unfit people I know! My feet hurt with each slap against the hard, uneven ground, and my body starts to flag quickly as I scramble for a place to hide. A big guy like that will probably catch me easily. Injured or not, he's on a rampage, and I'm his primary target.

Shit, he's catching up.

He's going to get me.

Kill me!

Veering right, I take a thin trail, plunging into thick foliage that looks as though it's grown over. This path must be old and unused. The plants are getting closer together. I slap them away from my face, whimpering and desperate as my view is obstructed. But I can't turn around. I can hear the man behind me!

Panicked breaths shudder through me as I desperately bash my way through the brush, nearly letting out a scream when I breach the foliage and find myself on the edge of a sharp drop. This is no small plunge. If I fall, I'm dead.

Taking a step back from the dizzying height, I scan the area and let out an uncertain gasp when I spot my path to escape. It's a rickety bridge that looks like it belongs on the set of a *Jumanji* movie.

"Oh, no way," I breathe, licking my lips and inching toward it.

That thing does not look stable. The rope holding it together has this green mold kind of stuff growing on it, and the planks of wood look like they could snap under the weight of a child, let alone a full-grown adult.

Maybe I could go another way.

"Where are you?" the man's voice thunders behind me.

I yelp and sidestep to the bridge, knowing that any second this man is going to bust out of the brush, see me, and finish what he started. I've pissed him off now too, so he's even more hyped up.

I reach the bridge and grip the posts anchoring it to this side. One of them gives a little wobble, but I don't have time to lament this fact, because the trees start shaking and the man appears, blood smeared across his face, enhancing his already frightening scowl.

He raises his gun and I bolt, getting five steps before the board beneath me snaps. My foot shoots into midair, my body quickly following as I trip and land on the bridge. It swings and sways beneath me, and I can't help a terrified scream as I gaze at the massive drop below.

"Oh crap, crap, crap." I'm crying the words, my body trembling as I pull my leg back onto the bridge.

I might crawl to the other side, but I'm paralyzed with terror, which is only made worse when the man joins me on the bridge. His laughter is dark and menacing as he pulls a blade from his belt. "Shooting you would be way too easy," he taunts me.

My entire body freezes up, shaking muscles turning taut. I can't freaking move!

"Just stay there, sweet thing. I'll come get ya."

Closing my eyes, I dip my chin and grip the board beneath me.

My stomach jerks with silent sobs. I'm a lamb to the slaughter, and I'm even more scared of what he might do to me before he finally takes my life.

The bridge sways beneath his weight, jolting up and down like he's running to grab me. I scream and lurch to the side, the moldy ropes catching me but giving me zero comfort.

I'm gonna die! I can't watch! I can't watch!

As I wait for my body to either be grabbed, or stabbed, or start plummeting for the earth below, I hear a weird grunt behind me.

My eyes pop open before I can stop them, and I dare to move and look over my shoulder.

The man is jerked back roughly, a flexing forearm tight around his throat. He lets out a strangled gasp and is flung backward. The entire bridge bounces as he loses his balance, then tips to the side. The guy beneath him grunts but does some quick leg move that has them spinning around.

The bridge continues to act like a theme park ride, and I scream, grabbing the rope and trying to stop myself from falling.

"Hang on!" someone shouts.

No, not someone… Cooper.

Lifting his fist, he smashes it down on the guy beneath him, grappling for control of the knife.

I should get up and help him, but I can't move! Terror

still has me in its talons, my fear of heights immobilizing me.

Cooper's muscles strain as he grips the man's wrist and tries to grab the knife off him. The men seem evenly matched in strength. Cooper grunts, executing a swift move that snaps his elbow into the man's cheek, dazing him enough to loosen the grip on the knife and… oh wow, he knocked him out.

When the hell did Cooper become such a ninja?

Jumping off him, the man I'm not sure I know that well anymore, rushes across to me and crouches at my feet. "Are you all right?"

I can't talk.

I'm still struggling with the whole having to move thing. My body is acting like granite.

Gently tipping my chin, Cooper inspects my face, a dark fury flashing across his expression before he goes to stand.

"Watch out!" I wail.

The second he moved, I spotted the man behind him. He's a mess but a freaking relentless one! Grappling with his gun, he tries to raise and point it, but Cooper's on him before he can shoot the thing.

An explosion of sound fires out of the weapon, and I scream, "Cooper!"

"I'm fine! Just hold the hell on!"

The board beneath him splinters as a spray of bullets fires between their legs. He jumps back just as another guy comes racing out of the bushes. He takes a moment to assess this crazy-ass situation, then launches himself onto the bridge.

Scrambling backward, Cooper shields me, gripping the knife behind his back.

"Are you holding on?" His question is soft and clipped.

"Yeah." Gripping the rope a little tighter, I try to figure out why he's asking me that question so much… and then he shows me.

With a move that's faster than lightning, he swipes the knife through the air, a series of sharp movements on either side of him.

What is he—

My stupid question is lost as the bridge goes slack, then starts to drop.

The sound coming out of me can only be described as a bloodcurdling shriek. It's what sheer terror sounds like, and I feel it all the way through my body as my worst fear comes true and I start plummeting into nothing but air.

Unprepared, the guys on the other side of the bridge flail and cry out in panic, their bodies falling like rag dolls.

It all happens so fast I can barely take it in.

My body smashes into the rock on the other side of the ravine, and my fingers give out.

"Ahhh!" I scream again, but the sound is cut short by Cooper's hand snatching my arm and breaking the fall.

"Grab the bridge," he instructs me, struggling to speak as he holds me with one hand and clings to the bridge with his other.

Swinging me back toward the rock face, he holds me until I've got a decent grip on the bridge turned ladder.

"Now, climb."

"It's gonna snap," I wail.

"I'm not gonna let you fall." His voice is so steady and confident I almost believe him. "The bridge will hold us. Now climb."

I hesitate, my stiff muscles still protesting my will to move.

"Climb, Ashlyn!"

Closing my eyes, I pull in a sharp breath and force my body up that ladder.

Cooper keeps his place, his hand locked around my arm until I've climbed past him.

I don't know how I do it, to be honest. My limbs are stiff and barely functioning, but somehow I make it to the top of the bridge and crawl onto the solid surface on the other side.

Slumping against the hard rock, I rest my face on the ground and pant like I've just run a marathon.

Cooper's hand touches my back, and I take in my first full breath. A relieved sob punches out of me and I roll onto my back, covering my face and shaking from head to toe.

"It's okay." Cooper's voice is a whisper in my ear. "It's okay. You're safe. You're alive."

His arm snakes around me and he pulls me against him, letting me shudder and shake until my shocked brain starts to function again. Rubbing my back, he presses his cheek against the top of my head and keeps soothing me.

After I don't know how long, my breathing returns to normal and I'm able to sit back and look at him.

"You came after me," I whisper.

His smile is grim, obvious pain and regret flickering across his expression.

"I couldn't do anything else." Gently touching my face, he runs his finger over my aching cheek.

I wince and hiss.

"Sorry."

I forgive his apology with a soft smile. "Where'd you learn to fight like that?"

He looks over his shoulder, obviously thinking about the men who fell into the ravine. "It's a long story."

I want to ask him more but sense this is not the time.

When he turns back to face me again, I take his hand and raise it to my lips. Kissing his knuckles, I open his palm and press my cheek into it. "I don't think I can do this without you."

His thumb brushes across my lips, the hard calluses on his fingers a heady contrast to my soft skin. Rough but gentle. Guarded yet kind.

I look into his eyes, the soft tenderness of his gaze melting away any lingering anger. All I feel in this moment is love. The love I've always felt for him. It blooms in my chest, expanding throughout my entire system and then freaking going off like fireworks when he whispers, "You won't have to. I'm here, and I'm not leaving your side."

27

THIS ISN'T DIE HARD

Cooper

THE SMILE she gives me makes me grateful for my promise. I just hope I can keep it.

The echo of those men's screams as they plunged into the ravine isn't going to leave me quickly. I wish I hadn't had to do that, but they were going to kill us. The bridge wouldn't have been able to hold all four of us for long, plus they were pointing a gun at Ashlyn. I'd managed to acquire the knife, which wouldn't hold off a man with a gun. I acted quickly, efficiently, and now two men are dead.

But Ashlyn's safe.

I check her face, that red mark on her cheek making

the anger surface again. When I first heard her scream, my blood ran cold. I'd already gotten up and started looking for her, but when I knew she was in trouble, something inside me snapped. I had to reach her, save her, do whatever I could to keep her safe.

"Should we keep walking? I have no idea where we are." Her voice still has a catch to it, a slight tremble that gives away her emotion.

I stand and help her to her feet. "I think I know, but let's aim for a high point so I can get my bearings."

She nods and trails after me. We don't say much as we walk, but the silence doesn't bother me. I keep glancing behind me to check she's okay. With each passing minute, she seems a little calmer, and by the time we reach higher ground, she's breathing steady again and has that bright, inquisitive look back in her eyes.

Shading my eyes against the sun, I do a slow circle, taking in the view below me and realizing exactly where I am. I thought I was in this place, but I wanted to double-check before leading us back into the brush.

"The resort's that way." I point northeast, knowing it's there even though I can't see it right now. "And the cove with the fishing boat is that way." I point west.

Ashlyn nods and climbs down from the rock, angling her body toward the resort.

I sigh and jump down, landing beside her. "Are you sure?"

Her look is so sweet and earnest, I nearly kiss her on the spot. "We have to help them."

"Leaving and getting help *will* help them."

"Please let's not do this again." She shakes her head. "I can't… I can't…" She sighs. "Don't make me fight with you. I feel about as strong as a fractured pane of glass right now, and I need you. Please."

I gaze at her, struck like I always am by this amazing woman. She thinks she's weak? Fractured glass? Yet she's willing to put her life on the line for her friends. Heck, she'd probably do it for innocent strangers too. She's always had the heart of a lion and the compassion of a mother hen.

How did I walk away from her?

Because you're not good enough for her, remember?

Knowing the truth, but also reckoning with the fact that I can't deny her, I hold out my hand. She takes it with a grin, and we make our way back to the resort.

My silent agreement seems to have shifted something within Ashlyn. I can feel a lightness in her, which is probably why she starts talking the second we hit the trail.

"Seriously, where did you learn to fight like that? I know your grandpa taught you a couple things, but you seem so quick, and efficient, and sure of yourself."

I scoff and shake my head with a short laugh. I don't feel sure of myself, but I don't think that's what she wants to hear. With a relenting sigh, I tell her the truth. "I worked in a gym for a while. The guy who owned the place was an expert boxer, and he got into martial arts as well. He used to let me train with him. I took lessons as a portion of my pay."

"You're good."

I shrug, not wanting to make a big deal of it. That time

helped me process a lot of shit. Everything was channeled through the training, and it released a lot of the darkness within me. Not enough to return to Montana, but enough to allow me to keep moving on with my life. The raging fire became embers I could live with, and I sought a new kind of peace—quiet, far away from city life yet nothing like the ranch. The island has been a place of solace... at least I thought so, until Ashlyn stepped off that boat and made me second-guess everything.

"So, what's the plan when we get to the resort?" I ask her, hoping for a subject change. The last thing I want to study right now is the history of myself.

"I have no idea." Ashlyn shrugs. "I mean, do you think we can somehow sneak our friends to safety?"

"Not likely." I wince, wishing I could give her a different answer.

"But we've already managed to get rid of two bad guys." I raise my eyebrows, and she snickers. "I don't know what else to call them. How many do you think there are? Could we like pluck them off one by one?"

I frown and shake my head. "This isn't *Die Hard*."

My memory flashes with an image of sitting on the couch one Christmas Eve, popcorn bowls on our laps as we boys watched the only Christmas movie we actually liked.

"This kind of feels like a jungle *Die Hard*," Ashlyn murmurs, and I can't help a smile. I love that she knows this movie too.

I hate to burst her bubble, but I have to be realistic about this. "I'm not John McClane."

"You practically are. You've got skills, and you're brave like him."

I stop, turning to face her with a pained frown. "No I'm not."

She looks confused and maybe a little hurt that I'd say something like that, but she doesn't know the truth. I'm surprised she even said it. She knows I left my family What's so freaking brave about that?

A shudder runs through me. I try to hide it by spinning and walking on, talking like I haven't just admitted I'm a big coward. "We could collect some intel. Maybe get a message to the outside that could help them. Numbers of men, weapons, that kinda thing."

"Do you know much about weapons?" she asks.

"Not really, but we could describe what they look like."

"Yeah, that could work." Ashlyn's voice perks up. "You know the resort pretty well, right?"

"Been working here for two years. I know this island. I've explored every inch of it."

"Two years? Here? Where else have you been?"

I glance over my shoulder and try to smile, but I'm sure all she sees is something I don't want her to.

"Man, we have a lot of catching up to do." She winks at me, trying to turn my frown upside down. She always used to tease me about how serious I was and how one of her purposes in life was to make me smile.

Damn, she always could.

My lips twitch and I take her hand, giving it a gentle squeeze. "So, we sneak back in, gather whatever information we can, and then sneak out again?"

"Yeah. That's a plan, right?"

I'm not sure how good it is, but yes, it is a plan. I like it better than the idea of her trying to charge in there and start freeing hostages.

"I know you don't love this, but I just can't leave them. How do I justify escaping to safety when their lives are in danger?"

It's nearly impossible to breathe as I choke out the words, "You can't."

28

HE'S STILL IN THERE

Ashlyn

AND MY HEART is breaking again.

The look on his face... the regret, the pain, the—

He didn't want to leave his brothers, but he did. And he's never gotten over it.

"Why? Why'd you go?"

"I had to." He swallows and looks away from me. "I'm not a good person, Ash, I'm not—" His sigh is heavy. "Let's just get this done, and then..." His jaw works to the side. "And then you never have to see me again."

"But I want to see you." I step around him so we're standing face-to-face. "God, I have missed you so much. When Aunt Nell told me what happened, I dropped everything. I didn't want to believe her, so I skipped a week of school and came up to see you. I couldn't believe you'd gone. That Ray was dead. That... my favorite place on earth was..." My lips start to tremble, and I can sense the onset of tears again. Sniffing, I try to rein them in as I touch Cooper's cheek and whisper, "The Cooper I knew wouldn't leave his family."

He pulls my hand away and takes a step back. "I'm not the Cooper you knew. I wish I could be, but I'm not. I can't ever be that person again."

And there's that pain, remorse, regret. He can't hide a speck of it from me. He's trying to be so silently strong and stoic, but I know this man. Yeah, he may have changed some, but...

Killing the space he created, I step right up against him, holding his face so he can't escape so easily. I search his eyes, letting him see how much I mean everything I'm feeling, then rest my lips against his. It's a tentative brush at first, but the second our mouths connect, that familiar sense of home washes over me and I linger for longer than I probably should.

Cooper goes still beneath my touch, like he's not sure what to do about this. But then his hand finds a place on my hip, his fingers lightly squeezing just before I pull away.

I can't help a grin as I study him. His gentle gaze warms with a smile I've known and loved for nearly half my life. Running my fingers over his ear and around the back of his neck, I lean my forehead against his and whisper, "You're in there. I don't know what you've done and why you hate yourself so much, but you're there. I wouldn't be feeling what I am right now if you were completely gone."

He squeezes my hip again and goes to step away, but I tighten my grip and kiss him one more time. I've finally got him back, and the thought of letting him go again actually hurts. I don't want to lose him, but I can't force him to love me back, and I don't know if I have any chance of changing his mind.

He seems pretty set on hating who he's become.

I just have to make him see that a guy as good as he is can never completely lose himself.

29

A WARRIOR

Cooper

SHE WOULDN'T SAY those things if she knew the truth. She wouldn't be kissing me and making me feel like I'm worthy. She doesn't know what I did! My choice. My callous, heartless, ruthless choice.

Nudging her hips back, I break away from the kiss, trying to soften the move with a smile. I know she'll be disappointed that I'm not into this.

Truth is, I am.

Man, her body is...

And those lips are...

Everything in me wants to lift her off the ground and have those luscious legs wrap around me. I want to run my hands over every inch of her body, remembering the feel of her bare skin beneath my fingertips. She was my first, and the only girl I've ever been with.

She's the one.

And yet I can't let myself have her, because she deserves more than a hate-filled killer.

I'm not that guy she thinks she sees.

I mean, I want to be.

I'm trying to make up for my past, but what if I snap again? I didn't think twice about cutting that bridge and letting those assholes fall to their deaths. What the hell does that make me?

How can I possibly be the person I once was? The one Grandpa Ray believed in?

He called me a warrior when I was a kid. I used to think it was kind of cool...

His gaze was so sincere, so full of pride, I could barely look at it.

"I know life hasn't been easy on you. Four little brothers, and a father who took out his rage on you. Life has turned you into a warrior. A guy who fights for the innocent. You've done everything in your power to protect the twins. They never got beat up, and that's because of you."

"Couldn't save Deeks or Michael though," I muttered, embarrassed by the compliments. I wasn't used to words of praise.

"You did what you could, and you're doing it again, allowing me to take you in, take care of your brothers."

I shrugged. "Didn't know what else to do."

He reached for my shoulder and I flinched. It was instinct. My muscles turned to springs when anyone tried to touch me. Grandpa lifted his hands in surrender and gave me a pained smile. "It's gonna be all right, son. I would never hurt you. I know you've been here less than a week and you're still finding your way, but please understand that you're safe. You can trust me."

I swallowed and tried to nod, but my head was stiff.

His smile grew, a short, breathy chuckle coming out of him. "Besides, I know better than to take on a warrior like you."

I frowned, confused. "I never fight back."

"But you could." He nodded, pointing at my chest. "You have a strength within you. It's quiet but solid. If you wanted to, you could be a force to be reckoned with. The thing is… you don't seem to need to do that, and that, my boy, is what makes you the strongest of us all. You have the ability to control your emotions, and that'll take you a long way."

———

I didn't control them that night I pulled the trigger. I aimed that gun and let hate, rage, and every beating my father had ever inflicted on me take over all my senses. It was pure hate that made me squeeze the trigger. I became the opposite of what my grandpa was proud of, and I don't know if I'll ever get over it.

A warrior is honorable.

There was nothing honorable about me that night.

I should tell her, so she understands. But I don't know how I could get the truth out of my mouth. We hid my father's murder, and I've kept it buried, locked within while I try to make up for my crime. I should have gone to jail, but my brothers protected me. I was supposed to be protecting them! And then I left. Didn't even say goodbye, and two of them nearly died! The twins got bounced around foster care. Did they end up with horrible people? They must have felt so disconnected and afraid.

I did that to them.

Pain tears through me like an earthquake, but I have to hold it in.

"Cooper," Ashlyn whispers, her eyes wide as she sees something in me. "Are you okay?"

I'm about to shake my head and say no when a noise to my right makes me flinch.

"Well, where the hell are they?" someone barks, but it sounds like the voice is coming through a radio.

"I don't know, boss. They're not responding."

"Find them! Fucking find them!"

I snatch Ashlyn's hand and start to run. I'm going back the way we came, which yes, takes us farther away from the resort, but we can't sneak back if we're caught, right?

Sprinting down the path, I drag Ashlyn behind me, trying to formulate the best escape route. Images of the island tear through me, and like a photographic map forming in my brain, I place where we are and where we can run to.

"This way." I yank her to the right and nearly trip when her hand suddenly leaves mine. Her soft cry of pain makes my blood run cold.

Did he get her?

Was she shot?

I didn't even hear a gun go off.

Spinning back to check, I find her on the ground, reaching for her foot with shaking hands.

"What's the matter?" I run over and crouch down, noticing how pale she is.

"I stood on something," she whimpers, her face bunching in agony. I reach for her foot and notice the gnarly stick poking into the heel of her foot. Damn, that's deep. It looks freaking sore. No wonder her tanned skin is turning white.

"I'm gonna have to—"

Footsteps nearby shut me up. I hear the soft crunch of boots as they navigate the path slowly, like they're trying to sneak up on us. Holding my breath, I tune my sense into the sound of his breathing, the soft click of his gun as he adjusts it in his arms. By the time he breaches the trees, I'm waiting for him, hiding behind a palm tree and ready to spring.

He spots Ashlyn on the ground and jolts in surprise, too distracted to even see me pounce. Grabbing the top of his gun, I punch out with my spare fist, dazing him before kicking out his knee and bringing him to the ground. I'm on his back and in full control as he lamely tries to wrestle me off him. A quick headlock and just the right amount of pressure has him passing out with minimal noise.

As soon as he's unconscious, I search his pockets, pulling out anything useful. I find a few zip ties and bind his wrists around a tree trunk, then use some dead flax leaves to bind his ankles. It probably won't hold for long, but it'll give us enough time to get away from him. Spinning him over, I disarm him and try to figure out how to unload the gun, but I don't know this weapon and feel like it'll be a waste of time to mess around with it. I don't really want to take it with me —I freaking hate guns—so instead I hurl it into a dense patch of foliage and pray to God it gets naturally buried over time.

Ashlyn softly whimpers, holding her foot and grunting in pain while she watches me work.

"How do you do that?" Her voice is strained.

"Do what?" I crouch back down to empty the last of the man's pockets.

"Fight so efficiently. Work so quickly. Act so calmly. I'm freaking out over here."

I stop to flash her a quick grin. "You're doing great. I'm gonna get you help, and this is all going to be over soon." Pulling the guy's radio off his belt, I wonder if I can change the channel and maybe signal a nearby boat. "How's your pain level?"

"I can manage."

"I need to get that stick out of your foot."

"There'll be a first-aid kit at the resort."

I cringe, wondering how the hell I'm going to sneak her into the resort and the office where all the medical stuff is when it's overrun with gunmen. But she doesn't want to abandon her friends. Shit. How do I play this?

The radio in my hand blips and I nearly drop it, but then that harsh voice is back. "Luther, come in. I want an update."

Staring down at the piece of hardware, I look to Ashlyn and silently ask for her advice.

She winces and shrugs, then mouths, "Respond?"

"Luther! Come in. I want an update on Cormac and Russell. Respond, dammit!"

Grabbing my shirt, I place it over the mouthpiece and make something up. "No sign of 'em."

"What about the runaways?"

"Ah… yeah. Found them. Dead. Cormac and Russ must have got 'em. They're probably heading back to you now."

"They're not back here or I wouldn't be looking for them, would I?"

I cringe, unsure how to respond to that.

The radio clicks again and he's yelling. "I want those bodies! I'm sending Rhett to help you carry them back. Give me your exact location."

I rub the T-shirt over the speaker. "Repeat?… Losing… can you…"

"Luther? Luther! Aw, shit!"

Lurching to my feet, I shove the radio into the pocket of my shorts, then reach down to help Ashlyn up.

She hisses and can't help a little yelp, so I sweep her into my arms and start walking.

"Where are we going?" She wraps her arm around my shoulders.

"I just remembered there's a fishing shed in a private cove nearby."

"But—"

"We'll get you fixed up, then head back to the resort to help your friends."

She smiles at me, and I swear the light from her eyes is like an energy burst. It feels good to have her in my arms this way. I used to love carrying her around. As soon as I knew she wouldn't mind, I'd pick her up whenever I could. It made me feel strong, capable, like I was the frickin' man.

And she's doing it again, without even trying.

I love this woman. I always will.

30

ALCOHOL AND PAIN

Ashlyn

COOPER CARRIES me along the trail, walking quickly and not saying anything. I don't either, not wanting to distract him or force him to talk back. He's strong, but he's carrying me a pretty long way. Maybe I should offer to go on his back. Would that be easier for him?

I glance at his face, affection blooming in my chest as I study that little frown of concentration denting his eyebrows and the tight pull of his lips. He's always been a serious guy, and I could always make him smile. That's why we worked. We were opposites with so much in common. Aunt Nell once told me that it's the perfect kind of relationship.

"Tom's as quiet as a mouse and I'm a barking dog. We complement each other, see? I can do all the talking for us, and he loves it that way. People sometimes think I married an old grump, but my Thomas is sweeter than apple pie on the inside. He's my other half, my soul mate."

I believed that about Cooper when I was young... and maybe I still do.

I've never had another serious relationship. I've never slept with another guy. Anyone who ever kissed me was always compared to Cooper. He was my first, and I want him to be my last. If only he'd let me.

I've got to break through whatever is holding him back.

Ah, maybe you should focus on getting fixed up and off this island with all your friends first!

I blink, forcing my brain back to reality.

"Are you okay? I'm not getting too heavy or anything?"

He snickers like that's a funny joke.

"I'm serious! You're having to carry me a really long way."

"I'm fine." His clipped words tell me he's not. I can see the strain on his neck muscles and the fact that he's starting to slow down.

"Cooper—"

"We're nearly there." He steps out of the shaded pathway and into brilliant sunlight, his body dipping to the side when we reach the sand.

I squint against the hot glow, the white sand of this peaceful cove working like a spotlight right in my eyes. My gosh, this place is paradise. A small cove looking out on the water. A fishing boat is docked about a hundred yards offshore, and there's a canoe that looks like it's been carved from a tree trunk resting by the palm trees lining the rocky embankment.

If things were different, this would be the perfect escape for an afternoon of sunbathing and skinny-dipping in the water. We could be the only people on Earth right now.

"It's beautiful," I whisper.

"Yeah, one of my favorite spots." Cooper hitches me a little higher and speeds across the beach, heading for a corrugated iron shed that's tucked in the very far corner of the cove, shaded by trees and no doubt home to all manner of island bugs.

Ew.

He places me down on an old-looking deck, treating me like cracked porcelain. "You okay?"

"Yeah." Taking my weight on one leg, I go to lean against the hut, then worry it might fall over under the pressure. There are gaps between the sheets of metal, and some of the pins holding this place together look to be missing or so rusted they'll fall apart with a flick of my finger.

The lock squeaks and grates as it's wriggled open, and then the door swings with a creak.

"Come on." Cooper reaches for me again, but I hold my hand up to stop him from picking me up. Leaning on his shoulder, I hobble into the shed and adjust my eyes to the gloom. "Take a seat."

I plop into the wooden chair Cooper pulls out for me. It squeaks and I hold the table, wondering if it's about to break beneath me.

Cooper's hunting through the cabinet against the wall and unearths an ancient-looking first-aid kit. I cringe when he places it on the table but don't say anything. His fingers shake just a little as he wrestles the old metal kit open.

"There's not much here," he murmurs, obviously disappointed as he pulls out some tweezers. "No disinfectant." He tuts, then gets up and hunts through the rest of the cabinets.

I finger the kit, noticing the serious lack of bandages and the few Band-Aids that look ready to disintegrate if touched.

"Yes. This'll work." Cooper sits back down, uncapping a small canteen and taking a whiff. "Alcohol."

I nod, then reach for it, taking a small swig and enjoying the burn of rum sliding down my throat.

"Good?"

"Yeah, it'll do." I pass it back, readying myself for the pain.

Gently taking my foot, Cooper rests it in his lap and inspects the wound again. The stick is lodged pretty tight into my heel, and the delicate nerves being assaulted are going nuts. I'm pretty sure this is the most pain I've ever been in, but I don't want to complain. I'm trying to be brave, in spite of the fact that I want to bawl like a baby.

Cooper reaches for the offending stick and I flinch, sucking in a sharp breath.

"I have to take it out."

"I know," I squeak.

His eyes soften with a smile and he caresses my ankle, those sweet hands of his sending crazy spikes of pleasure up my leg. "It's gonna be okay."

I nod, finding it impossible to talk. My throat is swollen with emotion, my heart racing out of time as Cooper reaches for the stick and pulls it free.

"Ow!" I screech. I can't help myself. My foot is officially on fire.

"Sorry about this." Cooper winces and douses the wound in alcohol, which nearly sends me through the roof.

"Holy f—" I bite my bottom lip, squirming to get away, but he holds my ankle steady and won't let up until the wound is clean. "Ahhh—ow!"

"I know. I know. I'm sorry."

"It's not your fault," I squeak. "You're just trying to help me." Tears burn my eyes and I squeeze them shut, not wanting to look at the blood that's now freely flowing over my foot and dripping onto the floor.

"Bandages, bandages," Cooper mutters, rifling through the kit.

I creep my eyes open. "I don't think there are any."

With a short huff, he pulls off his shirt, and that definitely helps in distracting me from the blood and quite possibly the pain.

He's so chiseled. That fine dusting of hair across his pecs—I want to run my fingers through it. I want to kiss the shape of his shoulders and the taut muscles that make up his torso. I want to run my fingers through the dips of his six-pack, tracing each ab until I've memorized the feel of them.

"You're amazing," I whisper, unaware that I said it out loud until he sighs and shakes his head.

"You shouldn't be thinking that."

"What?" I blink, then frown, annoyed by the fact that he's constantly putting himself down.

"I'm not... amazing. I'm not good. I don't deserve you."

"What are you talking about?"

He keeps his eyes on his T-shirt, winding it around my foot and ripping the ends to secure it into a knot.

Resting his fingers lightly over his handiwork, he traces the line of the cotton and sniffs. "Ashlyn, I... That night my grandfather died..." His voice trails off as he runs a hand over his head, mussing up the already messy waves.

"Yeah?" I can barely breathe. Is he about to tell me the truth?

Oh my gosh.

With a thick swallow, I lean a little closer, wanting to soak in every word.

"My old man. He showed up at the ranch."

My eyes bulge, knowing just how awful that must have been for them. "How did he find you?"

"I don't know, but he was drunk and raging."

"The beast." That's how Cooper always described him. His father had two sides—sober and depressed or drunk and raging.

"Yeah." He nods, squeezing the back of his neck, his forehead puckering into the deepest frown I've ever seen.

I reach for his arm, rubbing my thumb over the strained muscles. "What happened?"

"He pushed Grandpa. Shoved him against the fireplace. It killed him."

My mouth drops open.

"And then he was trying to choke Deeks. I walked in there with Grandpa's gun, and I ended it."

"You shot him?"

Cooper covers his eyes with his hand and nods.

All is quiet for a moment as I absorb this, picturing the scene in my head—the terror, the chaos, the all-consuming fear. Those poor boys.

"You saved them," I finally whisper.

He looks up at me, his eyes dark with pain. "I killed my own father. I shot him dead." His voice breaks. "He stole so much from me, and I hated him. In that moment, I *hated* him."

"You had every right to."

"Not to kill him. Not to hide it. We buried his body on the ridge and got rid of his car." Cooper's eyes glass with tears. He sniffs and starts blinking. I've never seen him cry before, and I doubt I ever will. This is pretty damn close, though.

Poor Cooper.

I can feel his pain, the angst. I wish there was something I could say or do to take it away for him.

"You did the right thing."

He shakes his head.

"You were brave. Courageous. You saved your brothers."

"Only to abandon them." He swipes a finger under his nose and looks to the floor. "I couldn't face it. What I'd done. What I had to do. I didn't think I could raise all four of them. Not without Grandpa. I didn't have it in me, so I took off." His forehead bunches. "I felt bad about it. It ate at me, so I came back and tried to see them, but they were all so settled, and I didn't want to disrupt that. I had to accept the fact that I'd spend the rest of my life alone. That's all I deserve anyway."

"Cooper." I shake my head, overwhelmed with sadness. How could he think so little of himself?

Lurching forward, I ignore the throbbing in my foot and wrap my arms around him.

He sits wooden for a moment, like he can't believe I'm hugging him. So I just squeeze a little tighter. Finally, his hands snake around my back and he holds me lightly, like he's afraid to cling too hard or it might break him completely.

31

NEVER AGAIN

Cooper

"IT DOESN'T HAVE to be this way." She strokes the back of my hair, her voice a soft whisper against my cheek. "They want you back. *I* want you back."

I pull away from her, unable to hide my shock, my surprise. "You heard what I just said, right? What I did?"

"Yes." Her calm, green gaze searches my face. "Every word."

"Then you know you could do so much better than me."

She gives me an emphatic look, like I'm both deaf and stupid. "I don't want better than you. You *are* the best. You always have been." Taking my face in her hands, she holds me steady and locks me in with her tractor beam eyes. "I told you, I haven't had one serious boyfriend in the last five years."

"That's impossible," I whisper. "I've seen the guys all vying for your attention. You could have anyone you want."

"I don't want just anyone." Her eyes, that face, it's so sincere. "Don't you understand? I can't get over you, Cooper Barrett. You're my person."

She can't be saying this.

She must not have heard my story properly.

I shake my head and whisper, "You want me? Even after what I've done?"

Her eyes light with a smile. "You are a *good* man. You shouldn't have to live with this burden anymore. Let go. Forgive yourself. Go home. Be with me. Give yourself a chance. I know you think you don't deserve it, but you do. Cooper, you do."

Her voice trembles and shakes, her words getting desperate as she climbs onto my lap and straddles my legs.

Pressed so close against me, I can't help but touch her. My hands ride the waves of her hair before encircling her waist. She gazes down at me, her green eyes a perfect ocean, clear and warm. Her lips like pink strawberries begging to be tasted.

I study them for a moment, tracing their outline with my eyes before claiming them. My body won't let me do anything else.

Running my hand up her spine, I meld her against me,

cupping the back of her neck and parting her lips with my tongue. She meets me breath for breath, her soft whimper of pleasure igniting an old flame that's never truly burned out.

The embers within me stir and pulse with heat as her tongue, her body, her beautiful soul stoke the dormant fire.

"I love you," she whispers into my mouth, igniting my heart. "I could never love anyone else."

I run my fingers into her hair, reciprocating those words with my tongue, my lips, my hands.

I need her. I've always needed her.

Walking away was the hardest thing I ever had to do, and now she's in my arms again.

I can't let her go.

I won't.

Never again.

32

OPIUM

Ashlyn

COOPER'S KISSES have always been intoxicating. His tongue has magical qualities that no other man on Earth possesses. Being locked against him, his strong arms holding me tight, his beard scratching my delicate skin— yeah, it's kind of addictive.

"Opium," I murmur against his lips.

"What?"

"You're my opium." I grin and kiss along his cheek-bone, then suck the sweet spot just below his ear before working my way back to his mouth.

The whiskers around his soft lips are a little spiky, but I don't care. I'm in Cooper's arms again. He's kissing me back, letting me in. After five years of my heart walking this place like a lost nomad, I'm back home, and it feels so safe, so good, so right.

I never want to leave this hut. I don't care that it's filled with spiders and other bugs. I don't care that it's falling apart. We can just live here in this little cove, catching fish, building a fire, making love in the sand with the stars twinkling above us.

The beautiful picture builds in my mind until it's so clear and perfect that I can almost make it reality.

Reality.

My friends.

The resort.

Hostages. Guns.

Fear.

I rip my mouth off Cooper's and sit back with a gasp.

His confusion is brief, morphing into a worried frown as he cups my face.

I don't have to say anything. He reads my mind just like he used to, and his eyebrows slowly rise with understanding. "We need to get back to the resort."

My eyes fill with tears as I brush my fingers along his hairline. I don't want to leave this moment. What if I never get it back again?

Resting his thumb on my chin, he lightly squeezes the side of my neck before pulling me in for a firm kiss. "We'll get back to this later."

I smile against his mouth and kiss him once more before reluctantly getting off his lap.

Cooper steadies me, clutching my elbow until I find

my balance. I rest my hand on his bare shoulder, electricity surging through me as I resist the urge to trace the lines of his torso.

Later, Ashlyn!

"Are you sure you're gonna be okay?" he asks. "I don't want you putting pressure on that foot."

"I'll manage. I can just walk on my tiptoes."

"I could get you out of here right now, then come back for—"

"I'm *not* doing that. I wouldn't be able to live with myself."

I wince, hearing my words too late and hoping I haven't offended him. He's finally let me in, and now I'm just throwing the regret back in his face?

He doesn't say anything, and I snatch a tentative look at his expression, but he's giving me one of his closed-mouth smiles. "You always were a tough one."

I want to disagree with him. I don't feel tough. The way I froze on that bridge, the fact that I couldn't even jump off that little waterfall. I'm a scared wreck, a lost girl who's been floating through life and being pulled from one direction to the next. I know Cooper has been battling demons, but at least he had a resolve.

I let his departure break me.

He let the pain from his past forge him into the man he is now. Sure, he's got some self-love to work on, but he's so capable. He's smart and humble and kind.

He's the best type of man, and I'm determined to help him see that.

And maybe, if I'm lucky, he'll help me find my way again too.

He'll teach me how to be that girl who climbed trees and didn't give a shit what anyone else thought. He'll give me the courage to finally work out what I really want to do with my life after college.

33

LOVE COVERS

Cooper

ASHLYN SAYS SHE'LL MANAGE, but I'm still worried about her. That cut on her foot is deep. She needs proper medical attention; there might be debris in the wound that could get infected. I have to get her to a hospital, but I know she'll never agree to that. Not without at least trying to help her friends first.

When we step out of the fishing hut, I fiddle with the radio, seeing if I can signal any boats nearby. But I get nothing but static. Not wanting to accidentally alert the assholes who have taken over the resort, I give up relatively quickly and slip the radio back into my pocket... but not before tuning it back to their channel so I can keep an ear on what's happening.

So far, things seem to be settled between them, but I'm just waiting for that moment when they discover Luther and go ballistic. They'll know I lied the second he's found.

Ashlyn hisses, losing her balance when she tries to find the most comfortable footing. She can't walk on that wound.

"Don't say it." She points at me. "I know."

With a resigned sigh, I turn around and offer her my back.

"Sweet man."

At least I think that's what she whispers.

Hoisting her onto my back, I get settled, finding the position easier than carrying her in my arms like I did before. She's not heavy, but walking like that for nearly a mile was tough. Having her on my back makes the trail easier to navigate, and we head back to the resort at a much quicker clip.

The weight of responsibility is a heavy one. It takes me back in time to the pressure I felt to look after my brothers, especially when Mom got sick. She didn't have to ask me; I just took it on board, making sure they got to school on time, breaking up fights in the playground that Deeks always got himself involved in, covering for Michael when he was too scared to come out of hiding, building the fort for Jake and Brody so they had somewhere safe to escape to. No matter what, I tried to cover each of my brothers and make sure they were okay.

But then I left them.

I thought I was so justified, yet they weren't okay without me. What the hell happened to Deeks and Michael, and why did that foster family bail on the twins?

I know I should go home to find out, but do any of them seriously want to see me?

"What are you thinking?" Ashlyn murmurs in my ear.

"Nothing."

"Liar."

I hitch her a little higher on my back and grumble, "You always could read me."

"Your shoulders are tensing up. Is it the resort or something else?"

"Just thinking about my brothers. You said they want me home, but aren't they angry with me? They should be writing me off."

Her breath is soft against my cheek as she sighs. "I think Jake's pretty hurt, and maybe Deeks is a little pissed, but they want you home. They just... they want to be a family again, and it's incomplete without you." She pulls my raggedy locks to the side and kisses the back of my neck. "They need you, Cooper."

And damn, if that doesn't feel good.

I don't want to be buoyed by that sentiment, but I've spent the last five years living for myself and somehow thought it'd make me feel better. But it doesn't. All I've been doing is digging that crater in my chest until I'm hollow all the way through.

"I know you think you don't deserve it, but they love you. You're family, and love covers. It covers all things.

Your brothers don't see it the way you do. They don't remember you as a killer. All they know is that you saved them from a beast that night… and then you disappeared. They don't understand why, yet still they want you home."

I swallow, her words causing a fresh ache I didn't even know I was harboring.

"They deserve answers, Coop. You owe them that much."

She presses another kiss to my skin and leaves me to think about it.

Images of the boys run through me—memories morphing into the idea of walking through that door again, seeing each of their faces, hearing their stories, hanging out with my own flesh and blood.

Grandpa always went on about the importance of family, and I let him down. Big-time…

"You boys need to stick together, no matter what. This here…" He looked around the table, taking Michael's and Brody's hands, then expecting us to do the same. We all linked together into a circle, and Grandpa nodded with a smile. "This is family. These are your people, and more might come into the fold, but this link must never be broken." His voice cracked, and Brody shot me an awkward look. I gave him a reassuring wink and set my gaze back on Grandpa. "I know what it's like to lose some-one. We all do, so you don't take this bond for granted.

You appreciate each other, you love each other. And even when one of you acts like an idiot, you forgive each other. This is your home, and I will do everything in my power to make sure it stays that way forever."

I broke it.

I let him down.

But I don't have to keep doing that forever. Ashlyn's making me believe there's a way. A chance. Redemption.

I really need to get off this island.

Focus, Cooper. Do what you can to end this crisis, and then get your ass home.

A blend of fear and excitement skitters through me, but I snap off the emotion, focusing on where we are and what's about to come.

Ashlyn's grip around my shoulders gets tighter when we reach the outskirts of the resort. I can see the edge of the white brick wall that borders the back of the staff accommodations.

I slow my pace, aware that any noise could give us away. Leaning against the wall, I slide Ashlyn off my back so we can do a quick recon and figure out the safest way in.

34

THREADBARE COURAGE

Ashlyn

THE BACK GATE we initially fled through seems to be unguarded, so we sneak in and creep around the staff apartments. My heart is in my throat as I limp beside Cooper, resting my hand lightly on his bare back. The muscles are tense beneath my touch—taut power on the verge of unleashing.

I can't believe how far he's carried me today. Surely he's exhausted, yet he'll never complain. Cooper has always been stoic. The strong, quiet type who won't hesitate to jump to someone's defense when needed. That's probably why he feels so bad about his brothers. He thought they were okay, that they'd be better off without him, yet they all ended up in dark places on their journeys home. He'll blame himself for it. I need to make sure he doesn't carry that weight along with everything else.

A shuffling ahead of us makes me flinch. I hold in my gasp, pressing my back against the wall and freezing. Cooper puts his finger to his lips and I nod, promising to stay quiet as he creeps ahead. He does a quick check around the corner, looking like a cop or a marine or something.

A warrior.

When he disappears and the scuffling grows in volume followed by a couple grunts, I know before I even get there that Cooper has downed another guard with efficient ease.

Limping up behind him, I take the gun he passes me and hold it between my fingers like it's about to bite me.

"I put the safety on," he murmurs. "I think."

I check the weapon and assume the little toggle I'm looking at is the safety. How do you know which way is on or off though? Bringing the gun closer, I see tiny letters spelling out "safe" and "fire."

Phew. We're good. I'm not going to accidentally shoot anyone, so I hold the gun like they do in the movies, resting it against my thigh and feeling weird. I've never been a fan of guns. There's way too much gun violence in America, so I've been anti-guns for years. Though Uncle Thomas has some hunting rifles, and I guess I'm okay with that.

"How many more do you think there are?" Cooper stands and starts dragging the unconscious man. Opening a dark green door, he shoves him inside. I peek over Cooper's shoulder and see it's a storage closet filled with cleaning carts and all manner of housekeeping gear. He looks around and grabs a thick branch from out of the bushes, shoving it under the handle to keep the door bolted from the outside. Then he glances at my hand, cringes, and gently takes the gun off me. I'm glad I don't have to hold it anymore, although Cooper seems pretty against them himself by the way he's scowling at the weapon. I understand why after what he told me.

His father was a drunken asshole, but killing your own flesh and blood. That's… I can't even imagine.

Resting my hand lightly on Cooper's arm, I squeeze his bicep and whisper, "I'm not sure how many men came onto the island. You've taken out five already, although the one from the apartment might have revived and be functioning again. So let's say four are no longer a problem."

Cooper glances over his shoulder at the door. "The one we tied up when you hurt your foot might be up again."

"You tied him to a tree. It'll be an effort for him to be running loose."

He nods, gliding his hand down my back. "How's your foot?"

"I'm okay." I force a smile. It actually freaking hurts, but I'm not laying that burden on him as well. "So, what are we assuming? A pack of six, ten, fifteen? How many people does it take to hold an island hostage?"

Cooper rubs a hand over his mouth. "I can only go by the books I've read and the movies I've seen, but let's try to figure it out. If every hostage is alive, we're looking at around fifty people, so there are probably two or three guards watching over them."

"And maybe four guards checking the perimeter?"

Cooper nods. "Then you've got the leader and maybe a tech guy sidekick."

"Are tech guy sidekicks still a thing?"

"I don't know." His shoulder hitches. "But the leader was definitely yelling at someone when we first checked out reception, asking for guests lists."

"Yeah, you're right. So, if we overestimate, we're dealing with about ten bad guys?"

Cooper tips his head, then gives me a thoughtful nod.

"Okay, so we're nearly halfway through them. Maybe only five to go."

His eyes narrow.

I grin. "Shall we get to work?"

"This isn't *Die Hard*," he reminds me. His look is so serious that it steals my smile and I have to bob my head several times so he knows I understand.

"I get it, I swear."

He points at me. "Recon. That's it. I'm not here to play hero and get us killed."

I nod some more, resisting the urge to tell him he is a hero and I think he could take out the entire crew single-handedly.

Biting my lips together, I quietly follow him down the path. My throbbing foot slows me down, but Cooper's nice enough not to rush ahead. I think he wants to keep me close. Thank God for that, because I seriously couldn't do this without him.

Sneaking around the back of the kitchen, we make our way through the thicker foliage, staying off pathways and collecting whatever information we can. One guard walks past us, an assault rifle slung over his back and a pistol in his holster. He scans the area, looking irritated by something before storming off. The bruise on his face tells me he's the guy Cooper took out in the apartment.

I start making a mental count.

Before we reach the corner of the admin building, we spot another guy sucking on a cigarette. He stamps it out with his foot as my brain snapshots everything I can about him—average height and build, black hair, earring in his right ear. Once he leaves, I follow Cooper to a hiding spot where we can see the glass doors into reception. I crouch down beside him, gripping his arm and breathing through my nose. The pain is climbing up my leg, my foot begging me to stop moving around and elevate already! But I don't have the luxury of doing that, and I don't want Cooper to know how much it hurts. He might bail on our recon plan, and I want to see my friends, make sure they're okay.

Cooper turns to check on me, and I force a neutral expression. Pressing his lips against my ear, he whispers, "I'm pretty sure there's an emergency sat phone in Maurice's office. I can't believe I didn't think of it before." His whispering grows terse with obvious frustration. "Once we scout the beach and island, I can sneak into his office and hopefully grab it. It'll be a way of contacting the outside."

"Sounds good," I murmur against his cheek.

Threading his fingers through mine, he leads me throughout the resort. It's a pretty rushed inspection of the property, and we don't even touch the far end, but what we spot from our hidden vantage points tells us the resort is being controlled by six men, not counting the ones Cooper has already taken care of.

Six. That seems manageable, right?

I swallow, limping back once more to the admin building and Maurice's office. We reach our target successfully and crouch below the window. Checking the coast is clear, Cooper leaps up and inspects the window.

I stand guard on one foot—a lame flamingo who can't really do much if someone does come around the corner. But I can, at least, warn him.

"I should be able to squeeze through." He eyes me up and down. "Although you'll fit easily."

"Okay." I wince. "Although I'm not really sure where I'm looking." Glancing down the walkway, I suddenly realize that if I take those stairs to my left, I'll be around the backside of the restaurant. I can hear the waterfall into the pool, and I can picture how it fits against the back entrance to the restaurant.

My friends are down there. I want to check on them. We managed a cursory look before, but I didn't get to actually see Leo or Shira. I just saw the tops of a few heads, and I don't know who they belonged to. I also want to see if any of them are injured or bleeding. How badly were they hurt when the guards were trying to "shut them up"?

We should probably get that last bit of intel before calling the authorities. Won't they want to know how many hostages are still alive and what state they're in?

"What's the matter?" Cooper touches my elbow.

"I just wanted to get an eye on my friends. Find out what kind of condition everyone is in."

Cooper looks past me to the concrete steps, then over my shoulder. "We already scouted the restaurant. They're in there."

"I know, but I didn't actually get to see them, make sure they're okay. What if you go get the phone and I sneak down that way?" I point behind me. "We can meet back here in five minutes, and I'll have even more information for you."

He's shaking his head before I even finish. "You're wounded and limping. I'm not letting you out of my sight."

"I know you want us to stay together, but I don't feel confident creeping into the office when someone could walk in at any second. I'll be trapped. At least you can defend yourself." He frowns, which means he knows I'm right. "No one is around here. I can easily sneak down, check on the restaurant situation more closely, and make it back here without anyone seeing me. If I do happen to get spotted, I can run and hide in those bushes over there or something."

"You can barely walk, let alone run."

"You know what I mean. I can hide in those bushes." I point to the foliage I'm talking about.

Cooper lets out a reluctant sigh. "If you have to, work

your way through that dense section on the left, all the way to the fence. Then you can follow that around to the staff quarters. There's an equipment shed right on the boundary where you can hide."

"Okay." I'm about to turn and leave him when he grabs my arm and pulls me back around.

"I don't like this."

I touch his sweet face, loving the protective look in his eyes. "I'll be all right. See you in a few minutes, okay?"

His swallow is thick before he moves without warning, pulling me into his arms and crushing his mouth to mine. The kiss is hot with desperation. I sink into it, fisting the back of his hair and silently begging the universe to not let this be our last.

We pull apart as quickly as we came together. It's a cold shock to the system, yet I manage a smile. My heart is putty, my insides melted goo. I love this fierce man before me. I want to tell him again... every freaking day for the rest of my life. It's what I've always wanted.

Please don't let me lose this chance with him.

"Stay out of sight, and be safe."

"I will," I whisper, giving him a quick peck on the lips before limping away.

I can sense him watching me and turn back at the stairs. His face is a picture of worry. I try to ease it with a confident smile. He doesn't manage to reciprocate, but he does nod and grab hold of the window ledge, climbing the wall and stealing into Maurice's office.

Hobbling down the stairs, I use the wall for balance and try not to make a sound. The waterfall masks the noises around me, but it's still a tense, edgy trip to the back of the restaurant. I pass the bathrooms I first saw Cooper in only two days ago and drop to my hands and knees. Crawling the last of the way, I find a small perch on the path below the window and lean against the wall, breathing in through my nose and trying not to pass out.

I have to take a look inside the restaurant. It's a huge risk. I could so easily be seen by one of the guards.

Mapping out my escape route, I imagine myself jumping down and clambering over the rocks that border the waterfall. I'll disappear into the bushes just behind that and keep going until I find the fence.

I can do this.

I can do it.

One. Two. Three.

I bob up and quickly scan the restaurant.

People are huddled in groups on the floor. A few are sitting at tables, but the majority are on the ground holding each other. I don't know how many there are, but it looks like the room is full, which means everyone must be alive.

Please let them all be alive!

There's a desperate air of exhaustion lingering over the place. I scan for Leo and see him next to Shira.

Oh thank God.

Ducking back down, I count again, then risk one more look. I need to check the position of the guards and that there are only three within the restaurant.

I count and take note of what weapons they're holding and how much of a threat they are. One is carrying an assault rifle, looking alert for action. Another is leaning against the wall, obviously bored. His arms are lightly wrapped around his gun as the barrel rests against his shoulder. The final guy is perched on the edge of a table, eyeing up Mel and Teagan like they're fresh pieces of meat.

Scum.

They squirm beneath his leering gaze, Mel reaching for Teagan's hand and giving it a squeeze while they keep their eyes focused on the floor.

My gaze darts back to Leo and Shira just as my best friend glances up. His nose is swollen, dried blood crusting below his nostrils.

Anger flares hot and fast within me. Those assholes hit my friend! They better not have busted any kneecaps. My eyes burn as I strain to see the rest of him, but then our eyes connect, and his miserable fear morphs into joyous surprise. His mouth drops open, his chin bunching before he holds the bridge of his nose and bursts into tears.

Shit.

His wails echo across the room, and I crouch back down.

"Hey! Shut up!"

Oh crap! What have I done?

Leo whimpers, obviously trying to contain his emotion. Shira is soothing him, and I think I hear Varam muttering to shut the hell up and keep it together.

"Don't be so mean," Shira snaps. "This is a high-stress situation, you asshole!"

"You can shut the hell up too!"

"Don't talk to her like that." Lance jumps in, and a small argument ensues.

I make my escape while the guards are distracted. I pray they hit Varam in the face this time and leave poor Leo alone. I pray he stops crying so he stays safe.

My friends are still alive. Relief pumps through me.

Hopefully their tiff won't change that status.

If they're being used for ransom, then it probably won't.

I have to keep believing that.

But I don't want them to get hurt again either.

Limping back to the stairs, I ignore the ache in my leg and make my way back to the meeting point.

When it comes into view, Cooper isn't there...and the threadbare courage I was hanging onto turns to vapor.

35

NOT ALL ORDERS CAN BE FOLLOWED

Cooper

CLIMBING through the office is freaking nerve-racking. When I find it empty, I ease in with a sigh of relief and crouch behind the desk. I can hear muffled voices through the door, so I work quietly, checking drawers and the low cupboard behind Maurice's desk. I find the phone after only two minutes of rummaging and then make a quick escape back out the window.

I land softly, wondering how Ashlyn's getting on.

I'm about to head for the stairs to check on her when I hear footsteps coming my way. Sprinting away from the wall, I dive into the thick foliage I pointed out to Ashlyn and scramble toward the fence line. Branches scratch my exposed skin, but I don't slow down, plowing forward like a machine.

My chest is heaving by the time I reach the painted cinder block. I lean my shoulders against the rough exterior and suck air in through my nose.

Shit! Ashlyn!

Ducking down, I peer through the trees and manage to make out a man coming around the corner. But then he stops, grabs the radio off his belt, and spins around. I wait another two minutes to make sure he's truly gone, then ease away from the fence line. I need to make this call and get Ashlyn before she's busted.

Keeping an eye on the admin block, I figure I'll jump out and snatch her to safety as soon as she appears.

The phone slips in my sweaty palm, and I catch it against my leg.

May as well dial now and start talking to someone.

I dial 9-1-3, figuring the Coast Guard is my best bet. I get through after only two rings and am soon speaking to an operator.

"Please state your emergency."

"Hey." I crouch down, keeping my voice low. "I'm on an island about thirty miles nor-east of Saint Martin. It's been taken by gunmen, and we need immediate assistance."

"Are you calling from *Paradis Idyllique*?"

"Yes."

"We're aware of the situation. Coast Guard and police

have been alerted. I'm transferring you through to the control center."

I check the wall beneath Maurice's window while I wait. Still no sign of Ashlyn.

Rubbing a hand over my mouth, I pinch my chin and start counting the seconds.

"Yes, hello, this is Captain Reid. Who am I speaking with?"

"My name is Cooper. I'm an employee at the resort. I managed to escape before the hostages were rounded up in the restaurant."

"Are you injured?"

"No, sir, but the person I'm with has hurt her foot. She needs medical attention."

"It's coming. Negotiations are underway. Hold on."

There's a horrible pause while I stare through the gap of trees, waiting for Ashlyn and now this Captain Reid.

He returns a moment later. "Cooper?"

"Yes, sir."

"Please state your full name, date of birth, and how long you've been working on the island."

I roll my eyes. *Seriously? We don't have time for this!*

I grudgingly share my details so they can verify my identity.

"Thank you," he murmurs.

Ignoring the pleasantries, I launch into the reason I called. "I'm not sure what you know already, but I can tell you that you're dealing with six armed men plus a few I've managed to—"

"Do not take matters into your own hands. You need to stay out of sight and safe."

"I understand that, sir, but I'm not about to be taken hostage. Now, the men on the island are armed with semi-automatic weapons—handguns and assault rifles, from what I can tell. One of them also pulled a knife, so they may have hidden weapons on them. There are two men in the reception area, plus others working the perimeter of the resort and three guards keeping an eye on the hostages."

"What is the status of the hostages? Any wounded? Dead?"

"I'm not one hundred percent sure of that. I only got a quick look at the restaurant where they're being held. We can get you more details, though."

"No, you sit tight."

I glance toward the admin building, hoping for a flash of Ashlyn, but I still can't see her.

Dammit.

"We're formulating a plan to make sure every guest and staff member on that island is safe. The hostage-takers demands are high, and we're working on stalling them until we can get into a good position. Promise me you'll stay out of sight and not try to take matters into your own hands again."

"I can't promise you that, sir."

"I don't want the body count to be any higher than it has to be."

"I understand."

"Where are you currently?"

"I'm hiding behind the reception block."

"And the hostages?"

I frown, annoyed that I have to repeat myself. "They're in the restaurant. They—"

A sharp scream cuts my words short. It's not nearby, but it's desperate. I can hear the fear even from this distance. Gripping the phone against my ear, I wait, unable to breathe as the dread in my stomach stirs to a frothing volcano.

Who just screamed?

Was it a hostage?

Is someone about to die?

A cry of pain has me jumping to my feet.

"Ashlyn," I whisper.

"Cooper? Are you there?"

I ignore the man trying to get my attention, leaving the line open and placing the phone against the fence. Maybe they can trace it or something. Not that they need to. They know exactly where we are.

"Hello? Excuse me?" His calls for my attention get quieter as I rush out of hiding and head toward the sound of that scream.

I don't even care that I'm exposing my location. All I can think about is getting to my girl, so when a guard rushes toward me, I don't hesitate.

Grabbing the barrel of his gun, I pull it down, thrusting the heel of my hand into his chin before he can pull the trigger. He staggers backward, and I use that momentum to drive him into the wall. He hits it with a crunch and barely has time to counter my onslaught. I flick away his feeble attempt at a punch, kneeing his thigh and bringing him to the ground, still in control of his weapon. Two punches later and he's a limp fish. I take the gun off him, hating the feel of it in my hands but knowing if it comes to Ashlyn's life, I'll use it without hesitation.

36

COUNTDOWN

Ashlyn

"STOP SQUIRMING!" The man yanks my hair, pulling it so hard my eyes start to water.

I scream again, struggling to get away, but my heel hits the ground and the pain nearly blinds me.

I didn't even see him coming. One minute I was rushing for the window Cooper climbed through, but before I could even get up the stairs, some guy appeared. He must have come from the bathroom or something—an unaccounted body on the island. The guard who is going to finish me, if the savage look on his face is anything to go by.

Yanking my arm, he pulls me through the kitchen and

out the back. I'm stumbling and unable to hide my pain. I trip over the doorframe, my knees slapping into the concrete, and a fresh new agony running through my legs.

"Get up!" he shouts, wrenching me off my feet and wrapping his arm around my waist.

His pincer grip on my stomach makes me want to hurl. I push against his muscly forearm but soon give up the fight and let him carry me to the reception area.

Flinging the door open, he walks in and dumps me on the floor like I'm a sack of flour.

"Ow," I whimper, rubbing my hip and rolling over so I can see the man glaring down at me.

"Found her, boss." The guard nudges me with his boot.

I would turn to snarl at him, but I'm kind of bound by heart-racing fear right now.

The "boss" man in his brown combat boots is assessing me with a dark gaze that makes my skin crawl. Crossing his arms, he sniffs and bends down to inspect me. "There was no one else?"

"Found her outside the restaurant, sneaking around."

The man keeps eyeing me up, looking at my bandaged foot, which is now red with blood. "You sure she's the one?"

"Who else would it be?"

"I don't believe it." He picks up my injured foot, poking the area around the wound.

"Ahhh!" I can't hide my pain. Spikes of fire burn the area, making my nerves writhe and protest.

"She's injured. You're telling me she took out a guard

and dragged his unconscious ass into a storage room? You telling me she beat up Carl? Don't be such a fucking moron! She's not working alone. Go and find whoever she was with and eliminate him!"

The guard flinches at the thunderous orders. The boss's sudden change from calm to enraged makes me duck my head, terror pulsing through me in waves so thick I want to throw up.

As the glass door swings open, the boss grabs my arm and hauls me to my feet. "You and whoever the hell you're with have been a real pain in my ass today."

I can't look at his face, the venom in his voice making me tremble.

"Where are my guys? Huh? What'd you do with them?"

"Let go of my friends and I might tell you." *Oh my gosh, I did not just say that.* The beat of surprised silence is not for him alone. It pulses in the air, and I hold my breath until he bursts out laughing. It's a short, hard sound that ends with him fisting my hair and pulling it back so fast my neck wants to snap.

"You trying to negotiate with me? Huh?"

My nostrils flare, a breath shuddering through me as fear takes back full control.

"You little rich bitches think you can do whatever the hell you want. But I'm not leaving here without my money! And I'm not playing games with you, little girl!"

His fingers dig into my arm as he gives me a painful shake. "Tell me where your partner is."

"I don't know." I shake my head.

It earns me a cracking slap across the face. I gasp, my eyes watering as my head is flung to the side. Breaths punch out of me, and I can't see through my tears as he shakes me again.

"Tell me now or you are dead, do you understand me?" Pulling a pistol off his belt, he presses it into my forehead. "I will shoot you dead if you don't start talking."

I whimper, a desperate squeak coming out of me as I close my eyes and try to think.

I seriously don't know exactly where Cooper is right now, and even if I did, I don't think I could say! He has to get home, and I won't risk his life.

Oh God, help me!

"I'm gonna count to five, and then I'm pulling this trigger unless you tell me what I want to know! You got that?"

"I don't know. I'm serious. I *don't* know."

He pauses, giving me an ominous glare before opening his mouth and starting to count. "One…"

37

A CHOICE

Cooper

MY FINGERS CURL around the gun as I lean against the wall and try to listen for Ashlyn. I hate the idea of her screaming, but I need a location.

Closing my eyes, I rest my head against the building and slow my breathing, tuning in to the sounds around me.

That's when I hear it. A cry of pain coming from my right.

Rage surges through me, dark and furious, the same way it did the night my old man showed up. For a second, I'm right back there, the chaos in the living room taking me out as I rush, gun in hand, into the middle of a crisis.

I was eighteen and panicking. The moment I saw my father, that emotion flicked to hate-filled wrath and I acted. I chose.

And I'm gonna have to choose again today.

The thought sickens me, but like hell I'm going to let these assholes hurt Ashlyn any more than they already have.

Covering my back with the wall, I head around the admin block, ducking out of sight when I spot a guard storming out the door, muttering under his breath. He doesn't notice me, but I wait until he's safely away before heading for the entrance.

Ducking down, I do a quick check through the edge of the glass and spot Ashlyn in some guy's clutches. He's gripping her too tight, shaking her, making her cry.

Shit! He's got a gun to her head.

"One."

He's counting.

He's frickin' counting!

Ashlyn whimpers, and it splinters something in my chest. Standing tall, I raise my gun and nearly take aim through the glass, but I can't risk hurting her. I don't know what the glass might do to the trajectory of the bullet, and I'm not willing to take that chance.

Flinging open the door, I punch through it and bark, "Let her go!"

The man stills, a look of manic amusement crossing his face as he grabs Ashlyn and pulls her against him. Wrapping his arm around her waist, he pinches her close, the gun still pressed against her forehead.

Her lips tremble, her wide eyes glassy with tears. I want to kill this man. I want to end him in horrible ways.

"Found you," he singsongs.

A red haze stunts my vision, my muscles vibrating as I grip the weapon and aim for his head.

"You gonna shoot me?" He chuckles. "You look like you want to."

I do. Dammit, I want to so badly.

But I can't risk hitting Ashlyn. This isn't like the night on the ranch. I had a clear shot at Dad's head, and I took it.

I can't do that here.

If I could, would I?

Gritting my jaw, a shaky breath fires out my nose, my words barely audible through my clenched teeth. "Let. Her. Go."

"See what we've got here right now?" The man's eyes sparkle like this is some kind of game. "They call this a standoff."

"You're gonna lose." I can barely speak past my rage. It makes my voice come out deep and gravelly. "This is over. Negotiations will fail. Authorities will storm this island. You will go to jail, and you won't see a penny of that money."

"Yes I will!" he roars, his face morphing to that of a wild beast's. Out-of-control rage. I've seen that face before, and I was always so afraid of it.

I killed because of my fear. My hate.

But I'm not that person anymore.

Pulling in a calming breath, I lower my voice and say again, "Let her go."

The man's expression changes even more, his lips forming an ugly scowl, and I act before he can.

Firing a quick shot into his exposed thigh, I watch him drop while Ashlyn screams and wrenches herself away from him. The gun in his hand falls and I flinch, worried it's about to discharge, but after the clunk, it goes still.

Ashlyn stumbles and crashes into the desk while the man writhes on the floor, crying in agony as he clutches his leg.

I race over, kicking the gun out of reach and crouching down to pistol-whip him in the face. I figure it's as good a way as any to shut him up, and I can't deny myself that small satisfaction. He pressed a gun against my woman's head. I should be beating the guy black and blue.

Dragging him around the desk, I use the zip ties I find in his pocket to secure him against its leg. Ashlyn has taken the pistol and is holding it steady in her hands.

"What's the plan now?"

"Help's coming." I grunt, lifting the man's legs around so they can't be seen through the glass.

"But there are still more guys out there."

"The leader's down. That's got to help, right? Cut the head off the snake and all that."

Ashlyn's worried frown is making my heart hurt. I wish I could hold her, reassure her, but this isn't over.

The door flings open and I pop up, armed and ready.

It startles the hell out of the guy who I recognize as Mr. Tech-Man.

I guess they are still a thing.

He raises his hands and stutters, "I-I'm unarmed."

"Get over here and make a phone call. Tell the authorities this is over."

"But…" He drops his skinny arms, looking around like he's waiting for backup.

"Your boss is no longer a threat to me," I inform him. "I'm in charge now, and you need to do as I say."

He frowns, hesitating on the other side of the counter, until Ashlyn pops up, pointing the pistol at him and softly demanding, "Do as he says. Now!"

Two guns pointing at his chest is obviously enough to get him moving. He jumps and leaps across to the desk. Spotting his boss's limp body on the floor makes him pale, and he nearly drops the phone when he tries to dial.

I lightly place the barrel of the gun against his shoulder, reminding him that I'm listening to everything he says. He calls the authorities, and with a little nudging from me and Ashlyn, he gives them every detail of his crew and their positions on the island.

The call comes to an end, and he doesn't put up a fight when I tie him to a chair, then head for the door.

"Where are you going?" Ashlyn hobbles after me.

"It's time to go and get your friends."

38

WAR CRIES AND TEARS

Ashlyn

I DON'T KNOW what Cooper has planned, but I hobble after him, in awe of the way he carries the gun, making it look like something he was born to do.

Calm and in full control, Cooper finds a position outside the restaurant and picks off the first gunman with a shot to the shoulder.

He falls with a high-pitched squeal, and the two other guards jump up as if they've been poked with a cattle prod.

Screams grow to a crescendo in the restaurant as the hostages duck their heads and huddle closer together, but they have nothing to worry about. The guards charge out of the restaurant with their guns raised.

I duck behind Cooper, gasping when I spin and find another guard rushing toward us. Acting on pure instinct, I flick off the safety and lift the pistol. Closing my eyes, I start firing, letting out a war cry as the gun jolts so hard in my hands I'm nearly thrown off balance. After the initial shock, I keep squeezing the trigger until the clip is empty.

When I creep my eyes open again, the man is lying on the ground, covering his head. I totally fired over him, but at least I protected Cooper's back. The man on the ground gets up slowly, his eyes bulging as he raises his hands. I'm surprised he's not firing at me. Can't he see I'm out of ammo?

I really must have scared him.

Wait.

What's that noise?

I look over my shoulder and finally register the helicopter hovering over the pier. Men in black rappel down to the wood, unclip, and start running toward us with their guns ready to go.

The island is soon swarming with navy officers and coast guards, and after identifying myself, I'm lifted off my feet and carried down the pier.

"She needs medical attention." Cooper carries me to the boat that's just arrived and places me in the hands of two paramedics. I reach out for him, desperate to keep him with me, but he's pulled away and disappears into a chaotic crowd of tears, wails, relief, and joy.

"Where are the kids?" he's asking. "Are they safe? Jazz!"

"Bembe's been shot!" She's wailing. "He needs help! He needs help!"

Cooper takes off running.

I try to strain and see what's going on, but I'm lifted onto the boat before I can. Leo and Shira come rushing toward me, Leo dissolving into tears the second his arms are around me.

"I thought you were dead," he whimpers, shuddering against me. "I thought you were dead."

Shira wraps us in a group hug, kissing my cheek and then Leo's. It's all too much and I'm soon crying along with them, the shock and horror of everything I just went through rounding over me like a tidal wave.

We cling to each other while the paramedics work on the more critical cases and I wait for my throbbing foot to be properly attended to. The longer I wait, the worse I feel. With zero food in my stomach and the adrenaline leaking out of me like I'm somehow full of holes, I'm about ready to faint.

Leo refuses to leave my side, and Shira only does because Lance needs a hug. I rest my head on Leo's shoulder and wonder where Cooper is. He'll no doubt be helping the injured, checking in with everyone, talking to the authorities.

I'll probably have to talk to them too.

I shudder, thinking about those bodies in the ravine.

"Okay, let's move."

I don't know who said that, but the boat engine roars to life, and we start shifting away from the pier.

"No, wait! Where are we going?"

"The injured need to get taken to the hospital. Your support person can stay with you, don't worry." A lady with a kind face pats my shoulder, but she doesn't understand.

I can't leave! Cooper's not with me!

Panicked breaths punch out of me as I scramble for the edge.

"Ashlyn! Stop! What are you doing?" Leo pulls me back from the edge, wrapping me in a hug and not loosening his grip until I've stopped fighting him. In the end, I curl against him and let the sobs rack my body, Cooper's name puffing out of my mouth on an incoherent whisper.

Leo cradles my head against his chest and shushes me. He's probably putting my behavior down to shock and trauma, and I don't have it in me to explain.

By the time we reach Saint Martin, my head is pounding so hard I think it might crack open. I'm ushered into an emergency medical center, where my wounded foot is properly treated. They're worried about infection and spend what feels like hours inspecting my foot and removing any debris.

It's a big hoopla, and I'm so over it. All I seem to be able to do is cry. I can't eat and end up puking bile into a bowl. They put me on a drip to replenish my fluids, and they must have put a sedative in there too, because I have no memory of falling asleep.

In fact, everything seems a blur, including the flight

from Saint Martin to JFK Airport in New York. I sit by the window, staring at the clouds and ocean below, numb to my core.

Cooper never came to Saint Martin yesterday, and we were rushed onto a plane this morning. Desperate parents are waiting for their babies to return home. The entire experience has put us all on edge.

When Varam tried to check on me before boarding the plane, I snapped at him, telling him to leave me the hell alone.

He jolted back like I was a crazy person, but I took it one step further anyway.

"Are you blind? I'm not into you, so stop trying!"

It shocked the crap out of those around me, and Varam hasn't approached me again. I feel kind of bad for the way I behaved, and I will apologize at some point, but I just want Cooper!

Leo's promised me we can contact the island when we get home. I tried this morning but had zero luck and ended up sobbing over my fruit salad at breakfast.

I'm a wreck, and I'm too damn tired to do anything about it.

Lance carries me to the wheelchair after the plane lands, and Shira pushes me through the airport. Leo walks with me, rubbing my shoulder and promising me everything will be okay. We're all still shaken, and Leo spent most of the flight trying to process the experience. He and Shira wouldn't stop talking the entire way. But I couldn't engage, even when they tried to ask me how I survived and what went down.

I gave them minimal details, and they soon gave up trying.

I'm not ready to talk about it.

I want Cooper!

"Mom!" Shira's voice breaks and she lets go of my wheelchair, breaking into a run and wrapping her weepy mother in a hug. Her father is right there beside them, welcoming Lance into the embrace and holding them tight.

I notice Leo's parents rushing forward too... and... oh my gosh, it's Scott.

Leo gasps, his steps faltering when he notices his ex-boyfriend approaching with tear-filled eyes.

Their embrace lasts the longest. I have no idea what Scott says to him, but Leo brushes the back of his head, and they share a brief kiss before finally pulling away from one another.

I roll the wheelchair forward in time to hear Scott saying, "When your parents called to tell me what was going on, I thought I'd lose my mind. It made me realize that I can't keep denying how much I miss you."

Leo's expression goes all mushy, and he wraps his arm around Scott's waist, leaning in for another hug. Man, I'm so happy for him, but the sweetness before me just gets a fresh wave of tears going.

They're interrupted by a phone call from my parents, who have been desperately trying to fly out of Vale.

"We're snowed in!" Mom's voice pitches. "Damn weather. I'm sorry, sweets."

"I'm fine," I murmur. "Seriously, don't stress. Leo's looking after me. I'll see you when you get back."

"We'll be on the first flight we can manage."

"You don't have to do that." I shake my head. "Seriously. Just enjoy the rest of your vacation."

"Ashlyn," Dad scoffs, muscling in on the call. "We can't do that when we know you're hurt. We're coming home. See you as soon as we can."

I hang up with a sniff and don't say anything as I'm lifted from the wheelchair and into the back of Mr. Zhao's Tesla. Leo sits with me, holding my hand and shedding tears of joy over Scott's appearance.

"He's following us back to the apartment. You don't mind, do you?"

"Of course not." I force a grin. "I just want to curl up in bed anyway."

"Aw, girl." Leo kisses my forehead, pulling me close and hugging me all the way back to our apartment.

39

IT'S TIME

Cooper

MY KNEE BOBS as I sit in Maurice's office, talking to the two police officers in lengthy detail about the events of yesterday. It's been a long twenty-four hours, and I'm done.

But I can't just walk away from this.

The only way I'm getting off this island is if I wrap up my business for good.

I'm not planning on coming back.

The thought sits way more peacefully than I thought it would.

Perhaps leading the authorities to the ravine and explaining about the two men they'd find down at the bottom helped, or perhaps it's the fact that everywhere I turn, I can see Ashlyn, yet I'm not with her.

I need to do something about that.

Maurice clears his throat beside me, his voice raspy when he responds to the next question. He's been pale and jittery all day, but I think he handled the entire hostage situation pretty damn well. His quick, calm thinking saved Bembe's life. The guy got out of surgery late last night, and he's going to be okay. Jazz is still with him at the hospital and won't be returning to the island for a few days. I'm hoping to catch them both in Saint Martin before I leave.

I glance at my boss as he explains how he negotiated with the hostages to let him give Bembe first aid treatment after they shot him.

"'He better stay down.' That's what they said. As long as none of my staff tried to come at them the way Bembe did, then everyone would be safe. But if anyone acted out of line, they'd start shooting. Some of the guests were punched and beaten for being too noisy or defiant, but no one else was shot." He rubs his forehead, blinking rapidly while a muscle works in his jaw.

Yeah, it's all starting to hit him now. I bet he's not going to be sleeping easy anytime soon. A trauma like this sits with you for a long time—lingering, jumping out to grab you when you least expect it.

Maybe I should tell him to take up martial arts. It definitely helped me.

I stay quiet as the interview continues. It's kind of

frustrating having to rehash this all again, but I guess they need exact details and witness statements.

"Cooper." The officer captures my attention. "Your actions, although dangerous, are commendable. You brought this situation to a close much faster than we thought possible. You saved a lot of lives."

Gripping my fingers together, I try for a smile, shaking my head and not really wanting the compliment.

I'm not a hero. At least I don't feel like one.

"These guys were amateurs trying to play a big game. They'd been following some of the guests on social media and knew exactly the clientele that would be on the island. After researching the resort, they figured they could raid it and make a billion dollars if they asked enough rich families for ransom money."

I wince, grateful I don't have any social media accounts.

The officer chuckles and shakes his head. "Criminals can be idiots, at least the unseasoned ones. Don't worry, they won't be raiding any more islands. In fact, they're gonna be in prison for a long time to come."

The female officer sits forward and smiles at me. "We had to deal with a lot of frantic parents yesterday, and I can assure you they are all most grateful for your help. I'm sure some would love to send you a personal note of thanks."

Shuffling in my seat, I grip the handle and murmur, "Could you…? Do you mind not sharing my details with any of those people? I'd rather just stay anonymous."

The two authorities look mildly surprised by my

request, but they both nod, their smiles full of appreciation.

Relief washes through me. Not only can I keep my privacy, but all the guests can now relax, knowing they're safe. The "bad guys" are going to prison. I'm sure everyone on the island will be pleased to know that too.

Maurice sniffs and covers his mouth. The guy will be crying tears of gratitude any minute now. I can sense it.

"You're lucky to have such a fine man working for you." One of the officers points at me, then looks me in the eye. "I'm sure your family will be very proud."

The comment stills me.

Grandpa. An image of his smiling face blooms in my mind, those proud eyes, that slight puff of his chest. Would he have praised my actions yesterday?

Yeah, he would have. He always knew you were a warrior.

I blink, the onset of tears unexpected and slightly embarrassing.

I shift in my seat, sniffing and trying to pull myself together.

"That's all we need for now. With this many witness accounts, these guys don't stand a chance. I doubt their cases will go to trial, so you shouldn't be required for anything else."

"Thank you." I stand and shake their hands, not slumping back into the chair until they're gone. Tipping my head to the ceiling, I let the exhaustion ride over me.

"You need some rest, my friend." Maurice pats me on the shoulder.

"We all do."

He lets out a self-deprecating laugh and nods. "I think I'd rather work. It's a nice distraction. But you…" He points at me. "Why don't you take a few days off? The next group isn't due until after New Year's… if they still want to come." He cringes, then shakes himself out of that depressing thought. "That gives you nearly five days. You can get off the island. Go do something to recover."

Go home.

The words are a soft whisper inside me, but my direction couldn't be clearer.

"Actually, Maurice…" I hesitate, knowing what I'm about to say will disappoint him, but I don't have another choice. I know what I have to do. "There's someplace else I'm meant to be. My time here has come to an end."

"An end?" He frowns at me.

"I've got to move on."

Maurice studies me for a moment, absorbing my news and obviously seeing something on my face that I can't hide.

A soft smile lifts the corners of his mouth. "Where are you going?"

Nerves skitter through me as I fight a grin and admit, "Home. It's time for me to go home."

40

THERE'S ONLY SO MUCH
WALLOWING YOU CAN DO

Ashlyn

I'VE ALWAYS LOVED my apartment in Greenwich Village.
Leo was renting it before I moved in, and his flair for interior design turned what used to be a boring square box into a tapestry of color and joy. It's like living in a rainbow, and it usually makes me feel so happy and alive.

Today, it feels cramped and cluttered, the explosion of color hurting my puffy, red eyes. My parents sit on the sofa across from me, their worried frowns and barrage of questions enough to give me a migraine.

I seriously want to scream and kick them out the door.
But I don't.
I stay in full control, giving them the details I know

they want to hear and leaving out the rest. Not that I have anything to hide, I just don't want to go into it.

All I want is Cooper.

I stayed up past three o'clock this morning telling Leo in full detail every little thing that happened to me while he huddled in that resort restaurant, fearing for our lives.

Scott sat up with us, holding his hand, rubbing his back when he cried, then holding my hand and passing me tissues when I couldn't stop blubbering over Cooper.

I tried calling the island again this morning but couldn't get through. I'm pretty sure they've shut down for a few days while they recuperate.

I wonder how he's doing. Thinking about him is all-consuming. I'm not sure how to contact him, to check he's okay.

Will I ever see him again?

The thought makes my eyes start to glisten and I blink rapidly to hide it.

"Aw, sweets, you've been through so much." Mom reaches for my hand, awkwardly leaning over the coffee table so she can squeeze it. "Are you sure you don't want to come home for a few weeks, just until you're fully healed?"

They asked me this yesterday when they first burst in the door to see me.

I refused then, and I'll refuse again today.

"Daddy can wait on you hand and foot." She grins, trying a new tactic.

But I shake my head, attempting a smile yet failing.

Dad flicks his hand through the air, obviously understanding more than my mother does.

"Leo's been doing everything for me." Keeping my voice light and upbeat is nearly impossible, but I can't venture into another debate about why I don't want to go back to their place.

This is my home.

Is it?

Ugh. I hate that doubt. I hate how displaced I'm feeling. This little apartment used to be my sanctuary. I don't even understand why I started feeling restless.

But now that I've seen Cooper, it's all changed. Or at least magnified my unrest.

I want him.

He's home for me, and maybe he always has been and I just didn't realize it. Maybe fate was preparing me to see him again, and that's why I've been struggling. I don't know.

"Well, sweets, you know our door is always open."

"Thanks, Dad." I smile at him, kind of hoping they'll leave soon. I'm not trying to be rude, I'm just exhausted.

Leaning my head back against the couch, I catch Leo's eye. My foot is resting on his lap. It's starting to throb again, and it's probably time for my next round of painkillers. I give him a weak smile, which he sees right through.

Turning to my parents with his special brand of honesty, he gives them a flash of his straight white teeth and says, "Well, it's always so great seeing you guys, but Ashy here is wiped out. I think she needs another nap."

"Oh." Mom blinks in surprise, then forces a polite smile. "Of course." Standing, she smooths down her woolen sweater, then walks around the table to give me a kiss on the forehead. "You take care."

Patting my shoulder, she then heads for the door and pulls my father behind her.

"We'll call you tomorrow." Dad waves, then closes the door.

I deflate with a sigh, grabbing Leo's hand and thanking him.

"It's okay. I can tell you just want to wallow. Entertaining guests is not conducive to that."

"I'm sorry for being like this. I just…"

"Wish Cooper was here?"

My eyes fill with yet more tears. Seriously! Why does this keep happening to me?

I feel like I've been crying for three days straight. I'm done now!

"I'm sure he's fine."

"Yeah," I croak.

"And you haven't failed his family. You tried."

I nod, thinking about the Barrett boys and knowing it's not my fault, yet still feeling like I let them down. I have to call Aunt Nell and update her, but I'm not sure I've got it in me right now.

Closing my eyes, I lean my head against the back of the couch and pray for oblivion to take me.

It takes me another whole day, but I finally find the courage to call my great-aunt.

"Oh, sweetheart. I can't believe it! Are you sure you're okay?"

"Yeah, I'm fine. My foot is healing, and I'll be back to normal in no time."

There's a pregnant pause that weighs a million tons before she finally asks, "And Cooper?"

"I don't know." My voice breaks. "I tried. I told him about his brothers and that they wanted him home, but then the island got taken over and... I don't know if I'll ever see him again."

"Aw, honey. It hurts, huh?"

"Yeah," I squeak, slashing tears off my cheeks. "I didn't realize how much I loved him until he was there. I don't think I ever stopped, and now it feels like I'm losing him all over again."

"He's your soul mate. I knew that from the first day you skipped in my door, practically floating. I asked you why you were so happy, and you just giggled and said, 'I made a new friend.' Then you giggled some more and whispered, 'He's the boy next door.' I didn't know which one you were talking about, but I did know my little ray of sunshine was gonna burn a lot brighter from that day on."

"I feel like a dull, gray piece of concrete right now."

Aunt Nell chuckles. "This too shall pass."

"I don't know. I'm so out of sorts right now. That's why I came to visit you over Thanksgiving. I'm just restless. Where am I supposed to be? What am I gonna do with my life after I graduate?"

"You know you're always welcome here."

"If it wasn't so freaking cold…" I snicker.

She laughs. "I know he's what really brought you back."

"Not just him," I assure her.

"Yeah, this place is pretty special."

I nod, melancholy swamping me as I stay on the line, not saying anything.

Eventually Aunt Nell lets out a soft sigh. "I really thought my prayers had been answered when you called me on Christmas Day."

I swallow, images of Cooper rushing through me, that new ache blooming in my chest again.

"I'm still not ready to give up, though. I just can't make myself believe that you saw Cooper for no good reason."

"I wish I could tell you he was coming back."

"I know. But you planted a seed in his head. Let's just give it a chance to grow."

I nod and sniff, licking my bottom lip and wondering if I should tell her why Cooper stayed away, what he did, how it all went down.

But I don't.

It's not my story to tell. Even when I was unloading to Leo and Scott the other night, I didn't breathe a word of Cooper's confession. I glossed over it, saying we talked about the past and then made out.

Touching my lips, I close my eyes and relive those kisses, wishing with every fiber of my being to experience that euphoria again.

There'll be no one else. How could there ever be?

"You take care, sweetie. I'll give the boys an update and tell 'em to keep those prayers coming. Cooper Barrett will step foot on his grandpa's ranch again. I'm sure of it."

I say goodbye and hang up, wishing I had my great-aunt's unyielding faith.

I'm not sure of anything right now.

"How's Aunt Nell?" Leo steps into the room, carrying two cups of coffee.

I take a mug with a grateful smile and adjust myself on the couch so I can sip it. I, inevitably, spill some on my sweater, and Leo rolls his eyes, heading back to the kitchen for a wet cloth. After mopping up the stain, he fusses with my foot, placing it on a cushion and then the coffee table. He's been the world's best nurse these past few days. I'm letting him pamper me. I think it's helping him deal with the aftershock of thinking he was going to die.

"So, Scott and I are going out tonight. Thought we'd get a little pre-New Year's Eve partying in." He wriggles his eyebrows. "Shira and Lance are gonna be there too. You should come with us."

I shake my head, wrapping my fingers around my mug and blowing on the hot liquid. "Leo, I can barely walk."

"Scott and I can swing you around. Your feet don't even have to touch the ground."

"I don't feel like it."

He groans and slaps the couch. "Girl! Don't make me lecture you."

I roll my eyes. "I'm fine. Just give me a few more days."

"You need to get over this moping. I know he's the love of your life, but maybe he's just not ready. And you can't sit around waiting for him to knock on the door. You need to get up and get on!"

I narrow my eyes and glare at him. "You cried in your bed for a week after Scott broke up with you."

"Yes, and you gave me the 'get on with your life' lecture and took me out dancing, remember?"

I frown at him, hating that I don't have a comeback.

"Ashlyn, I love you. You're my best friend, and I hate seeing you this way. I wish I could magically make Cooper appear. I wish we had a way of getting in touch with him, but the island's not responding, and you can't just sit around waiting."

"I'm healing!" I point at my foot in protest.

"You're stalling." He eyeballs me, and I have to look away.

Placing my coffee down with a huff, I run my hands through greasy hair and am tempted to hobble back to bed and hide under the covers.

But a knock at the door stops me.

Leo frowns, obviously wondering why our buzzer didn't ring first. Someone must have snuck into the building as someone else was leaving.

"Maybe Scott forgot his key," Leo murmurs.

I snicker and shake my head. Like that would ever happen. Scott's the most organized person we know.

Checking the peephole, Leo jumps with a gasp, his

fingers wrestling the locks open as he quickly unlatches the door.

"Well, hello, handsome."

"Uh… hi. Is, uh… is Ashlyn home?"

Oh my gosh, that voice!

I know that voice!

The pillow beneath my foot drops to the floor as I struggle off the couch and quickly limp around the coffee table.

Leo steps aside… and there he is.

My man.

My Cooper.

Tears fill my eyes, a wobbly smile taking over my face as he steps into our little apartment.

He doesn't say anything, just closes the space between us and lifts me off my feet. My legs automatically circle his waist like they were born to do it, and then my lips find his. Wrapping my fingers are his stubby ponytail, I'm transported home as he deepens the kiss and evaporates the pain in an instant.

His arms hold me steady, wrapping tightly around me as I cling to him like a monkey that can't let go.

Walking over to the couch, he sits down and leans back so he can tuck my hair behind my shoulders.

Gently holding my face, he drinks me in and whispers, "Are you okay?"

"I am now." I smile, then start to giggle like a schoolgirl.

I can't help it.

He's here.

Resting my hands on his shoulders, I explore the shape of them before leaning forward and pecking his lips. "I was worried I'd never see you again."

He winces. "Sorry it took me a few days. I couldn't stop thinking about you, but I didn't have your number or your address. Plus I had to pack up my life on the island and then—"

"Pack up?" I interrupt him.

"Yeah." He nods, his gaze thoughtful as he runs his hand lightly down my hair. "I'm going home, Smoky."

"You're…" A breath whooshes out of me, my stomach starting to shake. "You're going home?"

"It's time."

"Oh my gosh," I squeak, wrapping my arms around his neck and kissing his cheek, his ear, his neck. "Oh my gosh."

He squeezes me tightly against him, his hands running up my back as he softly whispers in my ear, "Wanna come with me?"

I sit back to check I heard him correctly.

Yep, those eyes are telling me I did.

Tears instantly line my lashes, and I'm barely able to see him through the blur.

He swipes the tears off my cheeks with his thumb, his vulnerable face achingly beautiful.

"Of course," I whisper. "I'll always come with you, wherever you want to go."

A slow smile pulls his lips wide, and without uttering a word, he tells me he loves me. His eyes are so rich with affection right now that my insides feel like helium. I swear, if he lets me go, I'll float right up to the ceiling.

I grin and nestle against him, tucking my head into the crook of his neck and closing my eyes for a minute. I just want to soak this all in.

He's here.

He's going home.

And he's taking me with him.

41

THE BOOK OF BARRETT

Cooper

AUNT NELL MET us at the airport in Missoula. I hugged her for the longest time, Ashlyn leaning against me and watching with tears in her eyes. Nell cried; heck, I nearly cried.

"You're home." She said it over and over. "He'd be so happy."

Those words were harder to hear than I thought they'd be. Guilt still clings like a toxic vine. My insides are raw and tender, yet I know I have to overcome this.

My brothers want me back. I have to at least go and see them, apologize, ask for their forgiveness.

We haven't told anyone we're coming. Aunt Nell

thought we should make it a surprise. I don't know if that's the best idea, but I'm going along with it.

As we near the long driveway up to the ranch, my gut clenches. Pressing my hand across my mouth, I blink rapidly when I spot the mailbox with "Barrett" written on the side. It looks like it's had a fresh coat of paint, and it takes me back to the moment I first saw it...

***

Since I was the oldest, Grandpa Ray let me sit up front for most of the trip. Florida to Montana is a long drive, but with every mile we got farther away from my old man, I felt the springs of tension unfurling a little more.

"Here we are, boys." Grandpa stopped at the end of the driveway. I nudged Brody's knee to wake him up. He jerked and blinked, his mouth dropping open as he took in the vast fields around us.

"You live here?" he asked.

Grandpa chuckled and accelerated forward. "I sure do. And I'm pretty glad you boys are going to be living here with me."

I trusted Grandpa, so the small flickers of doubt that tried to linger didn't have much strength. The second I stepped into the house, I knew we'd made the right decision. The sense of warmth that enveloped me. The sense of safety.

I took my time walking around the house, imagining my brothers in it and what we'd have to be careful not to touch. There were precious things on the mantel above the fire, so I'd have to make sure they didn't horse around too close to it. I paused to gaze at a family photo of Grandpa, Grandma, and my mom when she was a little girl.

"That's my favorite picture." Grandpa stepped over, taking the frame and lightly grazing his thumb over her face. "She was a sweet kid, and boy, was she tenacious."

His face crumpled with a look of sadness. It made me want to cry, so I blinked and quickly changed the subject.

"What does that mean?" I pointed to the frame hanging on the wall.

Grandpa returned the photograph and stared at the wall. "That's my father's family motto: 'Live justly. Love mercy. Walk humbly.'"

"Yeah, but what's it mean?" Jake chimed in, wriggling between the two of us and going on his tiptoes for a better look.

"It means you choose to do the right thing no matter how you feel about it. It means you show kindness to all people no matter who they are. And it means you do all that without getting a big head and thinking you're more important than anybody else."

"That's a lot to live up to," I murmured.

Grandpa just grinned at me and winked. "It's easier than you think."

Ashlyn's fingers curl around mine, bringing me back to the present. "It's gonna be okay."

I turn to look at her and she smiles, taking my face in her gloved hands and rubbing the whiskers of my beard. "You are a good man, and you deserve to be with the people you love."

It's gonna take some time for me to believe that, but I'm here. That's step one.

She leans over and gives me a kiss as Aunt Nell parks her truck next to the house.

Memories.

So many memories.

I step onto the cold dirt and scan the snow-covered fields. I always used to love this time of year. I mean, summer was the best... and not just because of the weather. I glance at Ashlyn and feel my heart kick out of place. But winter had a magical quality to it. Even though it could be miserable and cold, it was always so damn beautiful.

"Who you?" A small voice makes me spin, and I catch my breath.

That's something different.

A little girl.

Dressed in purple winter-weight sweats with unicorns and rainbows all over them, she stands on the porch staring at me with her curious big eyes.

"Hey. I'm Cooper." I raise my hand in a wave.

She points to herself. "Me Arwee."

I grin. Ashlyn told me she was a cutie. We've spent the last forty-eight hours glued together, planning this trip and talking about my brothers. She told me everything she could remember as I held her in the dark, worrying that it was all too good to be true.

"Arley's a pretty name."

She giggles, hugging her pink teddy bear and scruffy-looking rabbit.

"Hey, Arley." Ashlyn smiles at her.

"Hi, Ashwyn."

"You remember me?"

"Everybody talking 'bout you all the time, so it's hawd to fuhget."

Aunt Nell lets out a hearty laugh, clapping her gloved hands together before opening her arms wide. Arley laughs and runs down the steps, launching herself into an Aunt Nell hug. The old lady picks her up like she's nothing more than a feather, hugging her tight and grinning. "Aw, you sweet child. Who's home right now?"

"Arley?" An urgent voice rushes out of the house, a blonde lady appearing, wisps of hair flying around her face. "It's freezin' out here. You can't go keepin' the door open. It's—" She halts to a stop, her blue eyes bulging as she grips the laundry basket in her hands and yells over her shoulder, "Michael!"

My chest constricts, my heart jumping into my throat as I wait for my brother to appear. He runs out the door, obviously ready for action.

And not ready for me.

His steps falter and he ends up slipping on the icy porch. Landing with a thud, he winces, and I race up the stairs to help him stand.

Gripping his hand, I haul him to his feet. Before I can get a word out of my mouth, he wraps me in a power hug.

"You're home," he whispers, his body shuddering. "I can't believe it. You're home."

I tip backward, thrown off balance by the force of the hug. Slowly my arms encircle him, and my body doesn't know whether to laugh or cry.

"Okay, you two, take this inside. We're all gonna turn into ice cubes out here. Arley, come on, baby. Ashlyn, nice to see you again."

"Hey, Annie."

Michael drags me through the front door just as Brody starts thumping down the stairs. Oh my gosh, he's a man. Look at him. So freaking tall and muscular and... he's so... grown-up.

"What's going on down—" He gasps, losing his step but catching the railing before he falls. "Holy shit!" He starts laughing and vaults over the banister, landing with a thump and reminding me that he's still the youngest member of the family. "Jake, get your ass down here!"

I barely have time to respond before he's engulfing me. Brody's even bigger than Michael, and I'm lifted off my feet and spun around before being plunked back down on the hardwood floors.

Brody holds my shoulders and stares at me. I'm suddenly a billion-dollar painting in a museum. His eyes fill with awe as he shakes his head and squeezes my jacket, then touches the ends of my shoulder-length hair and scrubs his fingers through my beard.

"What? You gonna kiss me now?" I murmur, raising my eyebrows at the look on his face.

"I'm tempted, man." Brody laughs, his eyes glistening with tears. "Damn, it is so good to see you!"

He pulls me in for another hug, the embrace so fierce I can't breathe.

I slap his back and he finally releases me, wrapping his arm around my shoulders and steering me so I'm facing the inside of the house.

My eyes skim the dining table. It's cluttered with half-folded laundry, candles, and leftover water glasses. It's a damn sight better than the bare wood I stood in front of when I was last here. This house is so warm, just like when Grandpa was alive.

The cold chill that seeped into my bones when I stood in this echoing cavern has disappeared.

"No way." A young man's voice catches my attention, and I look up to the balcony.

Staring down at me is Jake, but he's a man now too. Far out, his face has changed. He's…

"Wow," I whisper.

He stays where he is, taking me in. The hesitant look on his face makes me want to cry, and I can't stop the tears from pooling in my eyes.

"I'm sorry," I croak.

It's all I can manage. If I try to say another word, I'll freaking lose it.

Pushing up his sweater sleeves, he descends the stairs, a slow smile forming on his face as he stands before me, then wraps me in a hug.

I hug him back, sniffing against his shoulder and apologizing once more.

"It's good to see you." He pulls back, slapping my shoulder.

"You too." I cup his cheek and start to laugh. "I can't believe how big you are. And, Brody, I mean… Holy crap, man. You're like a bear."

Ashlyn laughs. I turn to glance at her. She's swiping tears off her cheeks, just the way Nell and Annie are. I swear my heart is cracking wide open.

"Arley, what is it?" A man sighs from the kitchen. "Dee Dee's kind of busy."

"You gotta see this! You gotta!"

With a little huff, Deeks is pulled into the living area. The second he notices me, his mouth drops open. Ripping off his beanie, he holds it in his hand and gapes for a few long seconds.

"Hey, Deeks." I lift my hand in a wave.

He blinks, like the sound of my voice is turning this mirage into reality. With a little head-shake, he stares at me again and then starts to grin. "I can't believe she did it." He lets out an awed laugh and points to Ashlyn. "You did it."

"I told you she could." Michael crosses his arms, looking smug.

Ashlyn blushes and flicks her hand through the air. "I seriously didn't have to do much."

We share a knowing look. They don't know the full story. Oh man, it's going to be a long evening telling them. But after all they've been through, it'll be just another chapter in the book of Barrett.

Gazing around at my brothers, I feel the pain work through me. For a second, I can't look at them, my chin dipping as I squeeze the back of my neck.

A soft hand lands on my shoulder, then runs down my arm. Ashlyn's long fingers thread between mine, giving me the courage to speak.

"I didn't know…" I wince. "I didn't know what you guys had gone through. I thought you were okay, better off without me."

"What?" Deeks frowns. "Where'd you come up with that bullshit idea?"

I cringe.

"Dee Dee," Arley reprimands him. "Kena said no swears. You wanna do twenty?"

Michael snickers and covers his mouth before clearing his throat and giving me a serious nod. Deeks picks up the little girl and whispers in her ear. She hugs him and kisses his cheek. Then all eyes are on me again.

"I'm sorry it took me so long to get here. I'm sorry I left in the first place. After…after that night, I…" Anguish swamps me, cutting off my air supply and jamming my throat.

"You can do this," Ashlyn whispers. "It's okay. They love you."

I close my eyes and nod, speaking without looking at them. "I didn't think I could look after you guys without Grandpa around, and…and I… I killed—" My voice cuts off. Hot tears scorch my eyes. Ashlyn rests her chin on my shoulder, and I know what she's thinking.

Forgive yourself. Move on. Let go.

With a sniff, I swallow the lump in my throat. "I've got a lot of making up to do. I screwed up. And I'm really sorry."

No one says anything, so I creep my eyes open to check out faces. They're all the same—that torment from the night Grandpa died is running through all of us right now.

"You saved us," Deeks croaks. "You saved *me*."

I can no longer deny the tears. They spill off my lower lashes and I don't even bother to wipe them away.

"You don't need forgiving for that." Deeks clenches his jaw, tucking Arley closer like he's drawing strength from holding the little girl.

I nod, appreciating his sentiment, but… "I shouldn't have left. I'm sorry I didn't have the courage to stay." My voice disappears on the last word and I'm sure most of the room missed it.

Jake gives me a thoughtful nod. "Don't think there's anyone in this family who hasn't made a mistake before."

"Pretty sure mine's one of the big ones." I slash the back of my hand across my cheeks. I don't know if I've ever felt so weak and vulnerable before.

Deeks shrugs. "Even those can be forgiven, douche."

I snicker, giving him a grateful smile before flicking my hand. "Get your ass over here. Come give me a hug, you big idiot."

A sharp laugh punches out of my brother. Placing

Arley on the floor, he walks around the table and engulfs me in a bear hug that quickly turns into a scuffle. Brody can't resist getting in on the action. Michael and Jake make sure Arley is safely out of the way, and Annie pretends like nothing's going on and invites Ashlyn and Aunt Nell to sit down for a cup of coffee.

Damn, it's good to be home.

42

WHAT I WANT

Ashlyn

I STRETCH WITH A LUXURIOUS SIGH, then roll over and snuggle against Cooper's back. It's probably morning, but I don't want to open my eyes and see. It's warm under these cozy covers, and his body heat is just adding to the deliciousness.

With a sleepy groan, he rolls over and lifts his arm so I can nestle against his chest.

Brushing my fingers down his pajama shirt, I trace the raised pattern on the cotton and dare to open my eyes.

Yep, it's morning.

Cooper will probably have to get up soon. He's thrown himself into life on the ranch. Deeks had him working the day we arrived, but he walked in for dinner looking happy and relaxed. The evening disappeared as we met Kena, Indigo, Carmen, and Jackson, who arrived back from Harborton with bags full of groceries.

Carmen cried when she met Cooper, giving him a hug and saying something in Spanish I didn't understand. She's a real sweetheart. It's going to be sad saying goodbye to her and Jake tomorrow. Like me, they can't stay. Classes start soon, and they have to get back to Stanford. Just like I have to return to NYU.

The three of us will drive to the Missoula airport in the morning.

I shiver, hating that idea. I mean, it'll be great to see Leo and Shira again, but I don't want to leave this place! It's been the best five days ever. Watching Cooper come into his own has blessed my heart in big ways. He belongs in this place, and I don't even think he realized it until he got here. The brothers have so much fun together —laughter, jokes, hassles. And all the girlfriends are just divine.

Driving away tomorrow is going to be a killer.

I shiver again and pull the covers up to my chin.

"You cold?" Cooper shifts me a little closer, running his hand down my back and resting it on my hip.

I lift my knee over his thighs and half lie on him. I like the way our bodies fit together. Each point of contact is a little gift to the senses.

"How am I going to leave tomorrow?"

Cooper doesn't say anything for a beat, then softly sighs. "Well, I'm gonna kiss you long and hard, and then you're gonna get in the car. Jake's promised me he'll look after you."

I snicker and kiss his chest. "I'm not a little girl."

"No, you're my woman. And I know you can take care of yourself, but it's easier to watch you drive away when you're with people I trust."

I'll be on the plane back to New York alone, but I keep that thought to myself.

Running my hand over his chest, I tuck it around his waist and let out a happy sigh. "It feels right being here, doesn't it?"

He kisses my forehead. "Yeah. Thanks for telling me to come home."

"Thanks for listening." I look up with a grin and score a morning kiss.

It inevitably turns into something a little deeper, and Cooper lets out a moan of pleasure, rolling me onto my back and lying on me.

I giggle when his lips trail over my jaw and get that ticklish spot just below my ear.

He laughs softly against my skin. "Having you here too makes it just about perfect."

"Oh yeah?" I aim my dreamy smile at the ceiling. "What would make it *absolutely* perfect?"

Shifting his weight, he leans back so he can look at my face. His fingers are soft as they trace my hairline. "Grandpa Ray."

Oh, my heart.

Lightly squeezing his side, I give him a sympathetic smile. "Sorry he's not here."

"I can still sense him all around. Does that sound weird?"

"No. He's gonna live in your heart for the rest of your life."

"So are you." He brushes the tip of his nose against mine before dropping a quick kiss on my lips.

The smile in his eyes is everything, and I have to ask a question that's been on my mind since the day we arrived.

Scraping my teeth on my bottom lip, I study his expression and try not to let nerves get the better of me. "So, I've got six months left until I graduate. Do you think after I'm done, I could come back here for a while?"

His lips twitch. "Or maybe forever?"

I giggle, giving him a quick kiss and teasing, "You never got over me, did you?"

"I never wanted to." He chuckles, but his expression soon turns serious—sincere and heartfelt. I could drown in those eyes of his. "Smoky." He whispers my nickname and tendrils of pleasure curl through my body. "You're my one and only. Always have been, always will be."

I want to say so much, but emotions are clogging my throat and making it impossible to speak. So I show him instead.

Threading my fingers around the back of his neck, I pull him down to me, sinking into a slow, luxurious morning kiss that turns into so much more.

I guess we've got five years' worth of making up to do… and then maybe a lifetime.

Sounds good to me.

I finally know exactly what I want.

EPILOGUE

Cooper

THE SUN IS a hot beam on my head, but I soak in the rays, loving that heat.

"That's about it!" Deeks raises his hand, shouting across the field to let me know he's done.

I raise my hand in recognition, then head to the truck, gulping deeply from my water bottle before heading back to the house for lunch.

It's gonna be a full table today.

Jackson finished school last week, so he's around, which is super helpful, as Arley adores him and he's really nice about playing with her a lot.

That frees extra hands up to work on the property and paint the house.

It was in desperate need, but the job's a big one, so we've been putting it off. As soon as the weather started to shift in the right direction, we couldn't procrastinate anymore. We've been sanding and preparing the wood for days now. Kena and Annie are freaking Trojans. They work without complaint, and Indy pitches in when she's not doing her vet training.

Carmen and Jake are due any day now, and so is Ashlyn.

In fact, my beautiful lady was due last night, but her flight got canceled, and now I'm on hold, just waiting for her to call me. I'm desperate to see her again. Long distance sucks, and spring break wasn't enough. It was great having a full house over those days, but I wanted more time with Ashlyn, and we only got to sneak to the woods once.

I'm making up for it this summer.

Images of her luscious body naked in the private swimming hole make me grin.

Oh yeah, I am *definitely* making up for it this summer.

Jumping into the truck, I drive it across the field and pick up Jackson, who is waiting by the gate for me. I drive through and he locks it behind me before jumping into the passenger seat.

"Thanks, buddy."

"No problem." His body gets jostled from side to side as we hit a few potholes in the road up to the house. Yeah, I need to add road repairs to my list. Jackson rests his fingers on the dash to steady himself, and I notice how long his arms are getting.

He's on the edge of hitting puberty, and I think he's going to end up being tall and broad like Brody.

"Think I can take the afternoon off? Aunt Nell's invited me to ride the horses."

"That's cool with me, but you'll have to run it by Annie. She's the boss." I wink at him and we both laugh, knowing it's true.

His cheeks turn an amusing shade of red, and I just can't resist.

"Hailey's going too, isn't she?"

He clears his throat, his nose wrinkling as he stares straight ahead and doesn't answer me.

"You know, I met Ashlyn when I was thirteen."

"I'm not in love with Hailey!"

I grin, trying not to laugh out loud. He's scratching his neck and looking jittery, so I play nice and don't say another word.

The drive back to the house is quiet and peaceful. I really love it here. If I'd known how much peace I'd get from being around my family again, I possibly would have found the courage to return sooner. But it wasn't meant to be. And thank God I was on that island when Ashlyn was. The thought of her going through that terror without me keeps me up at night sometimes.

I'm so grateful she walked back into my life.

I wouldn't be here if it wasn't for her.

It's weird how life sometimes has a way of forcing your hand. Maybe Grandpa is up there looking out for us all.

We're home, and I think that's where he wanted us to be all along.

"Who's comin'?" Jackson murmurs, squinting his eyes and looking at the dust cloud forming along the driveway.

I lean forward and try to see if I know the car, but I've never seen it before.

Weird. We don't get a lot of visitors, and it always makes me antsy when we do.

Picking up the pace, I pull the truck to an abrupt stop next to the house and jump out, ready for action.

But then she steps out of the car, and my energy shifts to a whole different kind.

Smoky.

My walk turns into a run, and the second I'm close enough, I lift her off her feet and press her against me.

"You're home," I whisper into her hair.

She giggles, wrapping her legs around my waist and greeting me the way I've been dreaming about.

Our kisses make the rest of the world disappear, and I don't even hear my brothers unloading the car until Deeks shouts from the porch.

"Okay, we get it! You love each other!"

"Oh, let them be. It's cute." I can't see Kena, but I do wonder what Deeks is doing to her when she lets out a little scream, then starts laughing.

Ashlyn pulls away from me, always the curious one, and we turn in time to see him throw her over his shoulder and march into the house. Her protests are half-hearted and totally in vain.

"I guess we'll see them in a little while." I wriggle my

eyebrows, and Ashlyn's sweet giggle fills my heart. Then her expression changes to one of smoldering heat and my heart drops down to my knees.

"Maybe we should disappear for a little while too." She smirks. "I know this great spot in the woods."

With a little growl, I kiss her neck, then start carrying her toward the trail behind the house.

Her laughter is loud and rich as I place her on her feet and we run up the hill, arriving in the woods out of breath and on fire.

It's hours before we finally amble back to the ranch house, our fingers threaded together and my body buzzing with that tingling vibe only Ashlyn can give me.

"Thought you two were never gonna show up," Michael grumbles as we walk through the kitchen. Steam and good smells are rising from the pot on the stove. I lean over it and inhale deeply.

"I love your Bolognese, man. It's the best."

"Yeah, well, you can thank me later by looking after the kids so I can have some time with my lady. All of you took off to get happy while Annie and I were left on babysitting detail."

I laugh and slap his shoulder. "Got you covered, man."

"Thank you."

We walk into the kitchen to hollers and hoots. Ashlyn's cheeks flare with cute embarrassment. I just pull her against me and kiss her lips, then drop her into a dip.

Arley cheers and claps her hands. "Again! Again!"

Everyone laughs, and, as Grandpa used to say, *my cup runs over.*

As I sit at the head of the table, just the way he used to, I gaze around at the people filling the house and understand exactly how he must have felt. This house was an empty shell when I came back that time. It would have been just like that after Grandma passed away. Mom was in Florida and had cut her parents off.

But then she wrote a letter.

And he came for us, just like she asked him to.

In desperation, we agreed to go with him, and five scared, unruly kids walked into this house and knew they were safe.

He made us who we are today.

He turned us into Barrett boys, and now we're becoming a full Barrett family, just the way Grandpa probably dreamed of.

Taking Jackson's hand on one side and Ashlyn's on the other, we bow our heads to give thanks for the meal, and I whisper up an extra prayer of gratitude for this place and these people.

For my home.

Would you like to see what this family is up to a few years down the road?

Then get the exclusive epilogue novella: I Promise You...

Jackson promised to take his best friend to prom, no matter what. But four years down the track and things

between them have shifted. Can childhood besties become something more or will it ruin everything?

Jackson:

Lesson #1: When you're twelve and you make a deal with your best friend that you'll go to prom together, don't do anything to screw that up, even if she does try to seal the deal with a kiss.

Lesson #2: When things get awkward between the two of you, work your way through it and don't drift apart.

Lesson #3: When she starts dating some guy you don't like, don't be shy about telling her the truth.

Lesson #4: When her idiot boyfriend crosses a line, be the first to step up and protect her, because let's face it, she's the only girl you've ever wanted and maybe it's about time you tell her that.

I Promise You is a fun epilogue novella to wrap up the Barrett Boys series. If you'd love to revisit the Barrett ranch and check in with each brother as they help Jackson through the ups and downs of young love, then grab your copy today.

Available from your favorite online book store.

A NOTE FROM JORDAN

Dear reader,

I've always said Deeks's story - The Fighter - was my favorite Barrett Boys novel. Well, this one comes a very, very close second. I absolutely loved writing this book. Cooper and Ashlyn stole my heart. Their chemistry, their everlasting love, and the way they could no longer fight it gave me the biggest feels. I also loved Ashlyn's friends, especially Leo. He brought a fresh sass to the book, which was an unexpected surprise. But I think my absolute favorite thing about The Warrior is the family reunion at the end. The brothers are finally reunited and it is everything I wanted it to be.

This series has felt like a saga. I started planning for The Runaway over a year ago and it's been a journey of ups and downs trying to get these brothers back where they belong. But they did it. And my heart is full.

Thank you so much to everyone who has helped get me here:

Niki, Rachael, Beth, Kelé, Karen and Kristin. You are my constant sources of support when it comes to my books and I love you so much for it.

My review team - thank you for your enthusiasm over this story. It has seriously meant the world to me.

Thank you to my amazing Forever Love Crew. I love our daily interactions. You guys make this job so fun.

Thank you to my readers and for all the love you have shown these Barrett Boys. You guys are the best!

Thank you to Brenda who is always so full of encouragement. You are such a wonderful friend and I thank God for you every day.

And I can never finish a book without thanking my heavenly father—the creator of a love that knows no bounds and a grace that covers completely. I love you more than words can truly express.

xx Jordan

LOVE146

END CHILD TRAFFICKING AND EXPLOITATION

A way to give back...

I am passionate about telling stories of healthy love.
Unfortunately, there are some very distorted messages of
what love is out in the world today, and through my
books, I want to share the message of what real, good,
healthy love should look like.

A way for me to show this in action is by sharing my
profits with an organization that lives love on a daily
basis. Their mission is to eradicate child trafficking and
slavery from the world. They are truly an awesome
organization, and I thank you for helping me support
them.

www.love146.org

www.ingramcontent.com/pod-product-compliance
Lightning Source LLC
Chambersburg PA
CBHW020220260626
47156CB00002B/476